She heard an odd sound . . .

like a hushed burst of wind in the distance, and her eyes blinked open. The breeze was blowing from the west—from the direction of her lab. The smoke was coming from that same direction.

She raced through the library, the hall, the kitchen. Outside, the steps tried to trip her, grass tried to catch under her bare feet. Something cut her right heel, and the old cottonwood and cypress blocked her view. As soon as she skidded past the trees she could feel the heat.

Yellow flames were licking the white stone building. The door to the lab was not only closed, but there was a long board braced against the knob. Smoke billowed in huge gray clouds.

It was the board that riveted her attention, not because of why or how it had gotten there, but because Nick was trapped on the other side of that door. . . .

Dear Reader,

When two people fall in love, the world is suddenly new and exciting, and it's that same excitement we bring to you in Silhouette Intimate Moments. These are stories with scope, with grandeur. The characters lead the lives we all dream of, and everything they do reflects the wonder of being in love.

Longer and more sensuous than most romances, Silhouette Intimate Moments novels take you away from everyday life and let you share the magic of love. Adventure, glamour, drama, even suspense— these are the passwords that let you into a world where love has a power beyond the ordinary, where the best authors in the field today create stories of love and commitment that will stay with you always.

In coming months look for novels by your favorite authors: Maura Seger, Parris Afton Bonds, Linda Howard and Nora Roberts, to name just a few. And whenever you buy books, look for all the Silhouette Intimate Moments, love stories *for* today's women *by* today's women.

Leslie J. Wainger
Senior Editor
Silhouette Books

Jennifer Greene

Secrets

Silhouette Intimate Moments

Published by Silhouette Books New York

America's Publisher of Contemporary Romance

SILHOUETTE BOOKS
300 East 42nd St., New York, N.Y. 10017

ISBN: 0-373-07221-X

First Silhouette Books printing January 1988

America's Publisher of Contemporary Romance

Printed in the U.S.A.

Books by Jennifer Greene

Silhouette Desire

Body and Soul #263
Foolish Pleasure #293
Madam's Room #326
Dear Reader #350
Minx #366
Lady Be Good #385

Silhouette Intimate Moments

Secrets #221

JENNIFER GREENE

lives near Lake Michigan. Born in Grosse Pointe, she moved to a farm when she married her husband fifteen years ago. Jennifer feels that love needs both laughter and tribulations to grow. She's won the *Romantic Times* award for Sensuality and the RWA Silver Medallion, and also writes under the name of Jeanne Grant.

Prologue

Three Years Ago

Hands slung in her pockets, Laura crossed the yard to her whitewashed lab. In two hours the crew would arrive and a monstrously long workday begin, but not now. Not yet. Some rare mornings were as special as a secret, and this was one of them.

A heavy mist drifting from the river muted the rainbow colors of the sunrise swelling on the horizon. The whole world was hushed, and scents of wild roses and honeysuckle tangled in the air. Moss drooped from the giant cypress near the porch like an old man's beard, and even the peeling paint on the white antebellum mansion behind her had no power to disturb her.

Just for a few minutes, Laura refused to worry about peeling paint, the ten-hour harvest day ahead of her, even whether the old brailer was going to last an-

other season. Digging the lab key from her jeans
pocket, she turned it in the lock and stepped inside.

Automatically filling a beaker with water for coffee, she let her gaze wander to the forty-year-old Jakway Pearls sign over her desk. Just below that were
two shelves of books enclosed behind glass—biology
manuals, gemology and oceanography texts. Neither
the books, nor the fishing nets in the corner, nor the
spectroscope on the Formica counter would probably
mean a thing to anyone but her, but it represented her
world, her life.

She'd come so damned close to losing it. True, her
two successful experiments with cultured pearls hadn't
erased every debt, but the taste of solvency was delicious, potent and as alluring as a lover. Safe was a
terribly precious word.

Everything was finally starting to come out right
again. Except that the mortgage was still hanging over
her head like a noose, she still desperately needed this
season's pearl harvest to go well, and there were a
thousand repairs and costs and . . .

"You're already starting to worry again. Can't you
just let it all be for a few more minutes?" she said to
herself with a rueful smile. Sam called her a worry-
aholic. Maybe she was, and maybe a lazy hazy morning could tempt a woman into feeling secure, safe and
on top of the world confident. But illusions didn't pay
the bills and neither did daydreams.

Humming a lazy ballad hopelessly off-key, she res-
olutely unlocked her desk and file cabinet, determined to banish the sleepy mood. Harvest or not, she

had to find time today to test the water in Crader's Cove for acidity. Where was the pH kit?

Bubbles were just forming in the beaker when a tall shadow blocked the sunlight in the doorway. "Laura Jakway?"

An emotion close to instant fear skimmed through her veins. The man's vibrant low tenor obliterated the last hum of serenity from her system. Sam wasn't due to arrive until nine and no one else was ever around this early. Certainly an occasional stranger ignored the No Trespassing signs posted around the property, but not at sunrise. Not when she wasn't prepared.

Instinctively she raised her fingers to the buttons on her high-necked blouse. Once reassured that every button was latched, she lowered her hand and pivoted to face the stranger.

Her pulse picked up a wary beat. There were trespassers and there were trespassers. Of necessity, trade secrets were mercilessly guarded in the pearl business, but any self-respecting thief would hardly be dressed like this. His dark suit showed the expensive lines of a European tailor and fitted his tall lean frame with a certain elegance. If her trespasser was clearly no thief, he just as clearly didn't belong anywhere near a small backwater town on the Tennessee River.

She smiled at him both coolly and curiously. "Yes, I'm Laura Jakway."

The man stepped out of the sunlight and into the shadow of the doorway, dropping a polished leather briefcase at his feet. "I didn't mean to startle you." He extended a hand. "My name is Nick Langg. I'm not much in the habit of making business calls at sunrise, but over the last few weeks I'd all but given up trying to get ahold of you."

"I'm not often near a telephone at this time of the year," she admitted. If her first urge was to ignore his extended hand, generations of inbred Southern manners made that impulse impossible. His grip was cool and firm and she guessed he made a habit of establishing authority in a handshake. So did she.

The strength of her small hand seemed to surprise him. His dark eyes glinted with momentary humor. "You don't answer your phone, and you also don't seem particularly interested in reading your mail. I've written twice."

Her housekeeper, Mattie, handled her extraneous mail during the busy harvest season, a fact Laura wasn't about to mention. Mr. Langg not only attempted to show who was boss by that handshake, but to deliberately isolate the boundaries of man and woman.

She wasn't about to make too much of that short physical contact, but a woman who failed to respect the warning signs of danger didn't survive long. Not in this life. Laura sent him a quietly measuring glance.

He had to be close to ten years older than she was, and he was a disturbingly striking man. Thick dark brows hooded his eyes and his cheekbones were bold and angular. His posture advertised pride and a certain impatience, and no woman would have missed him in a crowd. He didn't have to flaunt his sexuality. His hair was thick and black, his skin a sun-weathered gold, and although nothing specific in his features suggested Eurasian, Laura guessed that he must have had an Eastern ancestor somewhere. A Tartar warrior could have had eyes like his, slate black, exotic, broodily compelling.

The physical look of a man might have moved her when she was a young nineteen, but five long years had passed since then. Character mattered, not looks, and Laura had met no man in a very long time who disturbed her as this man did.

Some men talked about their power. This man wore it. The lines around his eyes mapped some hard traveled roads. There was a vibrant, restless energy trapped behind a man forcing himself to stand still, silent, waiting for her to finish studying him. He wasted no smiles. He also wasted no time. His lazy quietness was deceptive; those brooding dark eyes roamed freely over her face.

The frown between his brows told her that he'd had expectations about the Laura Jakway he'd sought out this morning. Expectations she wasn't fulfilling.

That problem wasn't hers. A whisper of air tickled her nerves. Perhaps it was the scrape of that dominantly male tenor. Maybe he meant her no harm, but he definitely wanted something.

Water bubbled in the clear glass beaker, threatening to overflow. She turned quickly. Using a rag as a hot pad, she lifted the beaker to the counter and reached for a mug. "What is it you want, Mr. Langg? Since you know my name, you must have had some reason for tracking me down."

"Make that Nick, and yes, I was hoping you'd be willing to spare an hour to talk pearls with me."

Thoughtfully she reached for a second mug. "I'm afraid I don't have cream or sugar."

"I don't need coffee."

"I'm hooked on that first cup of caffeine in the morning myself." A spoonful of instant, and she had her palms wrapped around the steaming mug. A small army of nerves was collected under the surface of her skin the instant he'd said pearls. She would really be extremely happy when this man was gone, but she leveled at him her most genial smile. "Well, you're in the right valley if you're interested in pearls. Musseling used to be a major industry in the whole valley between the Mississippi and Tennessee rivers. My family was one of many who used to make their living pearling, but really, if you're interested in history—"

"No." When she lifted the mug to her lips, she saw his gaze wander briefly over her books and equipment, then return with upsetting intensity on her face. "I'm not a tourist, Miss Jakway—Laura—and natural pearls hold no interest for me. It's the cultured pearls I wanted to talk to you about. *Your* cultured pearls."

That, of course, wasn't possible. Any neighbor in the valley could have told Mr. Langg that her primary business was breeding mussels and that she also eked out a living on freshwater pearls. No one but Sam and Mattie knew about her experiments with superior quality cultureds. That secret was almost as well guarded as the reason she wore high-necked blouses. "I'm afraid you're in the wrong place," she said quietly. "Nat Hemming's only a few miles out of Silverwater. He's an expert on cultured pearls, and there's George Macklin a wonderful man over in Camden—"

His smile came from nowhere. "You have to be at least twenty years younger than I expected."

Laura glanced at her watch, feeling abruptly irritable. It was going to be interesting, kicking out a man who had nearly one hundred pounds on her. Interesting, not impossible. "Look, Mr. Langg—"

"Nick," he corrected again, and leaned back against her lab counter. "Three months ago, I saw a necklace in a jeweler's window in New York—a single strand of cultured pearls, valued at close to a hundred thousand dollars. I believe those were your pearls. The jeweler was Saul Rothburn, and I don't mind telling you that getting your name out of him had something in common with pulling teeth."

But Nick Langg had managed. He was the kind of man who would always get what he wanted, Laura thought dryly. Briefly she considered wringing Saul's dear neck and even more briefly considered denying that those pearls were hers. Both actions would have been wasted energy. Pearls of a certain quality were as unique as they were rare; any truly excellent pearl dealer could recognize their source by the look of them.

Saul was the best dealer in the business, and that necklace was the result of two experiments that represented the world to Laura. It was the culmination of five years of waiting, hard work and being terrified of the financial wolf at the door. Five years of breaking every known rule about the raising and breeding of mussels. Five years of searching for something in her life to hold on to.

Suddenly, her head filled with images of fire and loss. Grief was a wasted emotion, a luxury she'd never been able to afford, but sometimes...

Abruptly she felt the judgment in Nick's dark gaze. The stranger's inspection sent an unfamiliar feeling of vulnerability shivering over her skin—alien, intrusive, and fiercely unwanted.

She knew what he saw: a blend of silk and jeans on a slight frame that barely reached five-foot-four. Her hair was a swath of dark smoke that was simply brushed back from a delicate widow's peak to her shoulders. Black hair, magnolia-white skin and blue eyes set in small elegant features—surface beauty was the wrapped package. Men valued that so highly. She valued it not at all. If she'd had a choice, she would have picked a physical appearance that reflected the power of a woman's will and the drive and need to succeed that were dominantly part of her.

If her trespasser focused only on looks, she might not have minded. Really, only scant seconds had passed while he held that eye contact. Not long. Only long enough for her heart to suddenly beat *please leave me alone, Mr. Langg*.

"Maybe you'd better tell me exactly why you're here," she told him quietly.

"Yes." His gaze immediately shifted to his briefcase on the floor. Maybe she imagined it, but his tone seemed to change from crisp to gentling low. "I won't take up any more of your time than I have to, Laura." He raised the case to the counter and flipped its latches. "I came here to see if I could interest you in doing a project for me." His hand emerged from the open briefcase in a fist that he reached out to her. "Open your hand, would you?"

"I don't see—"

"Please, just look. Nothing else I have to say is going to make sense until you've seen these."

Claiming her hand, he gently opened her fingers, palm up. The current of contact sent heat shimmering through her veins. A platoon of butterflies settled in her stomach. Maybe he meant no harm. Maybe he was only a stranger with an honest reason for seeking her out, but she suddenly wanted him out. Away. Gone.

Seconds later, she completely forgot both that contact and the man. A dozen pearls lay in the cradle of her palm. They were perfect and, oh Lord, blacks. In sunlight, their luster caught her heart, her breath, her imagination. Each glowed. All pearls have a special glow when exposed to the warmth of skin, but this was more.

Her whole life was pearls, but the best she'd ever dreamed of producing were never this exquisite. In texture, color, luminescence, they were priceless. She turned each, her heart throbbing in excitement each time she lifted one to the sun. Each was alive. Only someone who understood pearls could understand that mystical quality of life they possessed. The best gems breathed, glowed, vibrated for touch, thrived on the softness of skin, dulled in darkness, exalted in light. None that she'd ever seen in her life was more precious than these.

Nick said quietly, "They're yours."

She froze.

"Not like that, dammit." Amusement sparked a flare of lightning in his eyes. This time when his gaze flickered over her, there was a trace of gentleness that was almost...intimate. "I seem to be doing a very good job of handling this entire meeting with the finesse of a schoolboy. Maybe I can do us both a favor and start over. A stranger barging into your morning, particularly when you're a woman and alone—in your shoes, I wouldn't be reacting with an overdose of hospitality myself. Blunt and sweet, Laura, I'm not here for you or your pearl secrets or to intrude in your life. If I'd been successful in contacting you any other way—but I wasn't. I've come better than two thousand miles to show you those pearls and to ask for your help. Will you simply listen, please?"

She raised her head, her blue eyes as still and as shiny as aquamarines. He started talking and pacing at the same time, touching a book here, a net, the blinds at the window.

"I'm afraid I have to waste a minute more of your time explaining how little I know about pearls. All I know are the basics most people are familiar with. Whether a pearl is natural or cultured, it's produced the same way. When any foreign substance intrudes under an oyster's shell, the creature's instinct is to grow a substance called nacre over it. Over time, the layers of nacre become a pearl. In natural pearls, that foreign substance could be anything—a grain of sand, a microscopic stone. But with cultured pearls, man deliberately embeds something under the oyster's shell—I believe it's called a shell nucleus. That's correct so far?''

"Yes." Those were textbook basics.

"Fine." Nick slugged his hands in his pockets. "So as a pearl grower, you try to affect the quality of pearls by managing all the variables you can—the temperature of the water, the growing conditions, the species and health of the mussels you use. I really have no idea what all you do, but if I understand the bottom line, a pearl grower can affect quality. But he has absolutely no way to *guarantee* the quality of pearls that come out of those mussels. Correct?''

"Mr.—Nick," Laura interrupted politely. "I learned the basic biology of pearls in diapers. If you would just explain the nature of this project you want me to do."

Unsmiling, Nick leaned back against the counter and motioned to her hand. "Those pearls are supposedly a product of an experiment that was tried once, more than forty years ago, and never repeated. Basically, a special nutrient was injected in the oyster's shell nucleus. And every oyster that was injected that way would seem to have produced only black pearls. Pearls as consistently perfect as those in your hand."

Relief, or perhaps disappointment, washed over her. Regardless, all the wariness tensing her shoulders completely disappeared. "That's not possible," she said simply.

"Believe me, I agree." He smiled wryly.

"I'm sorry, Nick, but someone's misled you." Calling him by his first name was suddenly as easy as the empathy in her voice. "Badly misled you. For one thing, there are thousands of mussel species, but only two or three that regularly produce black pearls. I'm not saying nature doesn't occasionally slip a black pearl in the other breeds, but we're talking once in a blue moon."

"So I understand," Nick agreed.

"And as far as some magic nutrient formula that could control the quality of pearls..." Laura shook her head. "Pearling is hardly a new industry—it's literally centuries old. Your idea is fascinating, but very honestly it must have been tried. I work on experiments with quality all the time. My facilities are terribly limited, but I study and read constantly, and my apprenticeship with pearls started when I was a very little girl with my parents. Believe me, there are no easy answers to good pearls. Real and total control of quality—it simply can't be done."

"I agree," he repeated, and then said slowly, "The pearls in your hand, though, came from that nutrient."

She refused to look down again. "They had to be a fluke. There's no other explanation."

He nodded. "Cards on the table?"

For the first time since he'd walked in, her smile came easily. "Cards on the table," she affirmed.

"I understood before I came here that the nutrient formula wouldn't—or couldn't—work. I still need it tested. If I could do it myself, I would, but I don't have the lab, the time, the expertise, the setup that you do."

"There are other cultured pearl growers in the area. Larger, more powerful ones. I already mentioned

George Macklin, and even closer is a man named Nat Hemming—"

His gaze lanced her face. "Yes. I investigated a fair list of names before I came here. No one fit exactly what I was looking for but you. Rothburn led me to believe you'd guard a secret with your life and that mattered to me. You have the skills to produce pearls like I saw in New York, but you're still small enough to do your own work. And there's the obvious issue of money." He hesitated. "I can pay you well for doing the project for me, but long-term the idea's worth no more than a pipe dream. You've even said as much. So I doubted I could interest anyone in doing the experiment for me who was solely motivated by money. I had to find someone who simply had a feeling for pearls, a love for them. And Rothburn led me to believe that you might be that person. Was he right?"

Silently, Laura damned Saul for his expansive tongue and wished she felt less helpless. "I can't," she said, not in answer to the question he asked but the one he was going to. A good businesswoman's blood had been flowing in her veins for five years. She had a work schedule ahead of her that would daunt most men twice over. She had no spare time, not if she expected to keep her head above water.

"I can promise you nothing." Nick's low tenor would seem to encourage her common sense. "Nor am I here for the hope of any profit for myself. The pearl nutrient was my grandfather's. No one—not in this life—could have loved pearls more than he did."

She found herself looking up at that odd catch in his voice. Grief? She knew the taste, color, texture of that emotion herself. "You're doing this for him?" she asked softly.

"All I promised him was that I would find a way to test his nutrient. It's a promise I have to keep, a secret I have to honor. I'll find someone else, if you're not willing. Believe me, I'll understand if you're not." His shoulders lifted with the simple question. "Yes or no?"

Sunlight washed silence in the small room. The question that seemed so simple to him was impossibly complicated for her. She'd heard everything he had to say. He'd said he was motivated to be here because of his grandfather, and she believed him. She looked at him and saw a man of power and pride, a man who was not finding it easy to ask a stranger for help. The way he moved, the way he talked, his clear bold gaze— honest men were not always comfortable to be around. They were also rare, and his integrity mattered. But it still wasn't enough.

Troubled, her eyes focused on Nick's. She felt no fear of him, but every instinct warned her against involvement in his project. Her stranger had secrets he wanted kept. So did Laura, and five years ago she'd discovered there were certain risks that were never worth taking. He'd walked in, and too easily she'd felt intimate feminine vibrations that were better left untapped, untouched.

But the pearls were so warm in her hand. She glanced at them again and her eyes softened helplessly. Schemes for fast riches could never lure her. Neither money nor a man had ever lured Laura. Even pearls in themselves could never have pushed her toward taking foolish risks, but the chance to grow perfect pearls was her dream. Her whole life.

"Yes or no?" Nick repeated.

"Yes." The word slipped out before she could stop it. She took a long breath. "But naturally—only if we can agree on conditions."

"That won't be a problem."

"No?"

If her drawl was pure Tennessee lady, she tested Nick with exhausting thoroughness for the next full hour. Her tone brisk and efficient, she covered contract options, terms, timing and the complex technical problems involved in his experiment.

He was silent, listening far more than talking, and soon the oddest smile gradually settled on his face. To an extent, that satisfied Laura. He hadn't expected a serious businesswoman and he'd thought her young. She could have told Nick that she'd earned respect from far tougher adversaries than a morning trespasser.

She could also have told him that the smallest argument would have given her the excuse to end the project here and now. But Nick gave her no argument. The payment he offered her was ridiculously generous and he abdicated to her judgment on everything that mattered. When he finally left, her lungs hauled in air.

Her nervousness was foolish. He only wanted someone to do his experiment for him. She'd reacted to a fear of something else, and when she opened her fingers, his black pearls were still damp in her palm. He'd refused to take them back. She guessed that to

Nick they were less a price for her services than brib-
ery for her silence.

He couldn't possibly know how unnecessary that
was—almost as unnecessary as her damp hands, her
thudding heart. Mentally she dismissed the nerves and
then the man. Neither mattered, any more than how
unlikely his project was. It was one chance in a million to grow perfect pearls.

From the time Nick Langg had started talking, she'd
really known there was only one choice she could
make.

Chapter 1

The Present

Get your nose out of that desk and get out of here."

Laura glanced up from the receipts on her desk and grinned. Sam was six-foot-four and edging toward fifty. His skin was like cracked leather and his looks were a cross between a Sherman tank and a gorilla. Both were prettier.

"We've been in full harvest for more than a month," she reminded him. "If I don't at least open these bills soon, someone's undoubtedly going to shut off the electricity and phone."

"That would probably be a blessing in both cases. Regardless, you're all done. If you don't have the sense to lock up after a twelve-hour day, I do."

Laura sighed, swinging out of her desk chair. "I'm going to fire you one of these days, Sam."

"I keep praying, but you never come through." He dangled the lab door key while she rifled the receipts into a file and drew the shades. Once he'd locked the door behind both of them, he tossed her the keys.

"Not that you deserve the invitation but there's probably enough dinner for an extra at the house."

He hesitated. "Who's cooking, you or Mattie?"

"Me."

Wordlessly he climbed into the driver's seat of his truck and turned on the engine. Laura propped her hands on her hips. "You survived the last time I cooked," she called out.

"Sure I did. I just never risk ptomaine twice in the same year."

Laura chuckled as he pulled out of the drive, and her gaze skimmed the lab grounds one last time. October was the peak of pearl harvest. Peeling flat-bottomed boats, smelly nets and awkward-looking cages littered the yard. Man-high mountains of shells caught a mother-of-pearl gleam from the late afternoon sun, and the pungent fishy smell was inescapable.

The yard looked a mess, but then harvesting pearls was a messy business. Always a critical perfectionist where her work was concerned, Laura had to satisfy herself that everything was as it should be before wandering toward the house.

The look of the white-pillared antebellum home inevitably eased her tired nerves and taut muscles. Bees drifted about the last of the roses. Dogwood and magnolia bordered the sides of the veranda, and the freshly painted pillars stretched up two stories.

The house and grounds were still a long way from being restored as Laura wanted them. The gardens were still wild, a new roof wouldn't wait another year, and more than one room inside craved a new coat of paint. Last year's pearl harvest had paid for the external paint project, but fast and total improvements still weren't financially possible. The fire that had taken her parents' life eight years ago had destroyed the entire west wing; smoke damage had affected most of the house. Laura had inherited minimal insurance, a mountain of business debts and the horror of this white elephant that had been in the Jakway family for generations.

But it was home. At nineteen, her entire world had crumbled because of that fire. She'd been told there was no chance of keeping her home...and had decided that there was no chance that she wouldn't. At the time it was all she had. One fought for what mattered.

And at the moment the only thing that mattered to her was a dripping cold glass of iced tea. She climbed the veranda steps, relishing those first moments of cool shade after twelve hours of working in Tennessee heat and humidity. A heat wave this intense in October was rare.

The cool hallway smelled of lemon oil and wax. She crossed the black and white checkerboard floor that led to an open wild-cherry staircase. White curtains fluttered on the cushioned window seat of the landing. She never failed to walk through the hall without feeling a luxurious wave of restfulness. Her lab represented her work, her dreams, the source of her energy and drive and strength, but this house was unquestionably her Tara.

Scarlett O'Hara never put together a peanut butter sandwich for dinner, she thought wryly. She was impatiently kneading a pinched muscle at the back of her neck when she took the first step into the kitchen and pulled up short. "Mattie! What are you still doing here?"

The face glowering at her about the frying pan was long, lined and dour. "I'm leaving, I'm leaving. Been trying to get out of this place for two hours, but that phone wouldn't stop ringing and then I knew darn well you'd probably starve rather than make your own dinner. Wash up and sit down here. If the chicken's dry, you got nobody but yourself to blame. Look at the time on the clock. Nearly seven-thirty!"

"You wouldn't have known I was late if you'd gone home when you were supposed to," Laura said reasonably.

Mattie sent her a telling glance. Telling glances had made up a major part of their relationship for the last four years. Laura had offered her old neighbor part-time work when Mattie's husband died. It was a terrible mistake on her part. Mattie was sixty-one going on one hundred and ten, unbearably nosy and exhaustingly bullheaded. What Laura would never have tolerated in an employee in her work crew, she ignored in Mattie. Her neighbor had no one. It was as simple as that.

Mattie motioned for her to sit down. "You got messages coming out of your ears."

"I'm listening." A mammoth plate of fried chicken and mashed potatoes appeared in front of her almost before she'd had the chance to rinse her hands. Four lumberjacks would have been delighted at the size of the serving. "It looks wonderful."

"It is."

Laura chuckled as she sliced into the succulent chicken, her gaze wandering over the old-fashioned kitchen. The room was a huge square with a neighboring pantry. The long tall cupboards were painted a French blue and the table was a well varnished oak. The built-in brick oven was over a hundred years old, and the raised hearth held a collection of copper kettles filled with wild flowers, pale blue and rose. Laura kept telling herself that when she had the money, she'd think about redecorating for more efficiency and space. She knew she'd never do it.

"Mr. Rothburn called, said he had a bid on those pearls you'd been waiting for."

"I'll call him—Mattie, there's enough here for ten. Why don't you stay and share it?" Mattie was tugging her purse straps to her shoulder, but she'd stayed this late, and Laura knew well she was going home to an empty house.

"Too many chores to do tonight. Did I tell you there was a key lime pie in the fridge? And there were more messages—the hardware's got some repair part you ordered. Hank Shull wanted to remind you about the barbecue on Sunday. Anna Lee said you owed her a lunch...."

"Hmm."

Mattie dropped a basket of six steaming rolls in front of her. "Don't hmm me. You haven't been off this place since the start of summer."

"Of course I have."

"For *work*."

"I've got all winter to be a social magpie."

"I know it's hard for you to believe, but the business won't turn to feathers if you're gone for a few hours. That Hank's a nice man. Some women around here just might begin to realize they're twenty-seven years old." Purse straps still swinging, Mattie filled the sink with soapy water.

"Is this the beginning of another lecture about landing on the shelf? How unusual. Mattie, cut that out. I'll do the dishes and clean up."

"You just eat. Nat Hemming called, too. That's the third time this week."

A quick frown creased Laura's brow. "Did he say what he wanted?"

"Nope. Just said he'd catch you another time."

For an instant Laura found herself staring thoughtfully at the clear gold tea in her glass. Everyone in the valley associated pearls with the names Macklin and Hemming. She didn't travel in either of their social circles, but Nat Hemming was her closer neighbor.

She knew what he looked like. She also knew he had ten times more money than he knew what to do with and guarded his mussel breeding secrets with tall fences and security guards. Privacy had to be fiercely guarded in the pearl business, not because it was easy to steal pearls but because it was too easy to steal techniques.

Her own techniques of breeding and nucleating mussels had yielded a third success—a third necklace that Saul in New York had sold for a wonderfully solid chunk of money. Fortunes, of course, were relative. It would take her more than an occasional necklace to totally change over her operation to farming the kind of cultured pearls she wanted to grow. In the meantime—until she had the money to pay for expensive security measures—there wasn't a soul in Silverwater who knew she experimented with cultured pearls. That included Nat Hemming. His sudden interest in her made absolutely no sense.

"Eat," Mattie scolded. "Nothing to get upset about because that old coot called."

"I'm not upset. I'm just well aware how much power Hemming has at the bank."

"He also chases anything in skirts, and at his age." Certain things settled a man's character for all time in Mattie's eyes. Pans washed and wiped, Mattie paused in the doorway with car keys dangling in her hand. "Nearly forgot. A Mr. Langg called, too. Said he was in town ahead of schedule and he'd be here by nine."

Laura's head whipped up. "Pardon?"

"Mr. Langg," Mattie repeated. Her feathery brows winged up at Laura's expression. "I figured from the way he talked you knew him. He seemed to take it for granted you were expecting the call."

"I was. Thank you, Mattie."

As soon as Mattie was gone, Laura could almost hear her heart go tick, tick, tick, in the sudden total silence of the house. Nat Hemming, tired muscles and money worries were abruptly locked in a distant corner of her mind.

She glanced at her watch, noted it was past eight and surged to her feet. Within five minutes she was upstairs and standing under the steady stream of a hot shower. The soothing pulse of water did nothing for her relentlessly climbing heartbeat. He was here. They were finally going to know if his nutrient formula had worked.

It had taken three years to test Nick's formula. Over that same period of time, she'd meticulously written him whenever there was a detail relating to his project that she thought he should know. He inevitably slipped a message back in the mail, usually nothing more than a bold slash of ''Fine'' scribbled on a single piece of paper.

Three years ago, she'd overreacted to a lot of troubling vibrations on meeting that man. His innocuous scratched notes had obliterated any lingering worries she might have had about working personally with Nick. He'd never questioned her, never commented, obviously never cared what she did. His letterhead indicated an import business with offices in Tokyo and San Francisco. More than once she guessed that he'd prefer to forget his whimsical project in a little backwater town in Tennessee.

She'd been the one to initiate their last written communication. At first, his blind trust in her had been a source of both reassurance and amusement, but later, irritation had set in. For her own legal protection, she wanted him there for his pearl harvest. She wasn't about to leave herself open to questions of theft or mismanagement—issues the darn man should have been worried about. She'd worried enough for both of them and insisted he come.

She knew he didn't believe in the formula. Rationally, she didn't either, but a corner in her heart stubbornly, blindly, willfully wanted to believe. A woman too hung up on being realistic and practical could forget the value of dreams. A very long time ago, dreams had sustained her when she had nothing else to hold on to.

Flipping off the shower faucets, she reached for a towel. Still dripping, she padded barefoot for her bedroom. Her pulse was suddenly slower, that bead of excitement subdued as she opened the drawer of her dresser.

Everything in the bedroom reflected Laura, a woman's private secrets, a woman's need for order and perfection. The walls were colored a pewter pink and the pastel carpet was soft and thick. Perfumes clustered in a corner of the dresser. Only a few small details marked this room as different from that of another woman who might have an equal love for pastels and soft textures. Her closet held hanger after hanger of blouses, all silk, all of a style that buttoned high at the throat. And there were no mirrors. Once, a mirror had been attached to the antique white dresser. Now, there was a charcoal sketch in pinks and grays and whites of a woman in profile: young, proud, alone.

Mindlessly she slid her arms in the sleeves of a pale rose blouse, her fingers avoiding the touch of skin as she buttoned it. Right after the fire, the scars on the right side of her body had been bumpy, hideous. Twice, a plastic surgeon had grafted. Now the skin was smoother than real flesh. The brand on her neck was no larger than a knife blade, but her right side and ribs were permanently red, permanently too smooth, permanently... ugly.

Only one man had seen the scars. One had been enough, and those were old waters over the dam. Swiftly, efficiently, she checked the top button of her blouse, slid into a jeweled print skirt and sandals and opened her closet door. On the top shelf, in an enameled box with a velvet lining that had once belonged to her mother, were Nick's black pearls.

When two of her own experiments had failed over the last three years, when a lemon of a day caught up with her, she'd taken out those pearls. The touch of them had never made a problem disappear for she'd never associated Nick Langg's project with any aspect of her real life. She'd just touched base with a dream, that was all.

Her fingers closed on the flawlessly smooth surface of the pearls. They were so precious, so lovely. And real. How could she not have invested a little hope that his formula had a chance of working?

Now the three long years of waiting were finally over. Her heart picked up a renewed beat of anticipation as she walked back downstairs to wait for Nick. His pearls warmed from the heat in her hand, and her sandals clicked as she paced the checkerboard hallway. Soon, she thought. Soon we'll know.

At five minutes to nine she heard the rap of knuckles on the tall Georgian front door. Spine straight, she moved swiftly to answer it. Pearls were the only thing in her mind when her hand turned the knob, yet for one long moment, the wash of sunset bathed Nick's tall dark form in color and shadow.

Her smile suspended, but only for an instant. Nerves pooled in her stomach that had no reason to exist. Then she stepped back and motioned him inside. "Come in, Nick. I'm delighted you could make it even earlier than we planned." She deliberately extended her hand.

"I hope it isn't an inconvenient time?" His palm enclosed her small one in neither a handshake nor a caress but exactly in the way he'd established physical contact before. His dark eyes glinted at her beneath the thick arch of his black brows, and there it was again. A three-year-old memory of uneasiness, excitement, confusion.

For his pearls, she reminded herself. "The time's just fine." Before he'd completely let go of her hand, she reached for his. What might have waited a few minutes suddenly wouldn't. Gently she slid the handful of black pearls into his palm and closed his hand over them. Out of sight, they were no longer hers and once given, any reason for further physical contact disappeared. "It's past time these were returned to you," she said lightly.

"I never intended for you to give them back."

"Yes, I know what you intended, and I never argued with you at the time because I always knew I was going to return them. You already paid me for the work I did for you. Pearls like these—even having them for three years was a payment of a kind." She smiled, stepping firmly away. "I thought we'd talk in the library. And if you'd care for a brandy..."

"It's not necessary." He glanced once at the pearls before slipping them into his pocket, and then his gaze traveled around the hall and staircase before returning to her face. "You have a beautiful home."

"A monster to keep up. Did you fly in?"

"This afternoon."

Which perhaps explained why he was still wearing a suit. The dark gray set off his broad shoulders, accented his striking looks. She remembered his black eyes. She remembered the hint of Eurasian blood that showed up in the proud way he moved, lithe and quiet and sure. She even remembered the curious blend of electric and remote about him—there was an I-dare-you-to-cross-me challenge about Nick completely at odds with an easy, almost lazy male confidence.

She'd completely forgotten that he was a man to make a woman feel vulnerable. He did it just by breathing, and her pulse was still humming errant rhythms that disturbed and confused her. She wished fleetingly that she was a cosmopolitan woman with a comfortable veneer of sophistication. She was twenty-seven years old and she certainly knew life. But not men like this one.

She strode ahead of him in the library, giving him a wide berth until he leaned back against the pecan desk.

"You wouldn't like to sit down?"

He shook his head. "I've been sitting all day." His gaze restlessly roamed the room, touching down on the long narrow windows that opened to her garden, the two long leather couches, the vase of roses scenting the room from the desk.

"Now that you're finally here, I hardly know where to begin," she murmured with a short laugh. "I prepared nearly a full notebook for you over the last three years, but it's down at the lab. I can get it for you later, if you like. I didn't realize you were coming until an hour ago."

He kept staring at those roses, and Laura heard herself distractedly talking faster. Her roses were such a foolish whim. Working out of the house all day, there was no sane reason to waste fifteen minutes in the early morning picking perfect buds that no one would even see. She realized it and still did it, inexplicably needing to know that the high-ceilinged room had a splash of red, the scent of warmth, something beautiful and feminine.

Those roses meant nothing to him, yet he kept staring as if they did. "I know I wrote you about the controls I put on our project, but letters never gave me much chance to explain those judgment calls." Briskly she talked up every care she'd taken with his experiment. She'd injected his nutrient into shell nuclei that were an exact seven millimeters in size. She'd only used young mussels, none that had been weakened by time in captivity. "I also nucleated an equal number of the same mussel species without your nutrient, so we'd have yet another control...."

His smile gradually unsettled her, and very odd feelings charged between blue eyes and black when she finally stopped talking. "By some remote chance, were you listening to a word I said?" she asked.

"Not really." His eyes were capable of a spark close to mischief that didn't seem to match his expensive tailoring, the control and authority so natural to him. His tenor scraped like the rough side of velvet. "Laura, I came to you because you have the expertise I don't have. You don't walk up to a chef and question his cordon bleu. There would have been no point at all in my seeking you out if I was going to doubt every decision you made."

"I have absolutely clear records of everything I've done. I've tried to set it up so you could check everything—"

"I'm sure you have."

She seemed to be amusing him. Vanity sparked a little flare of irritation. So, she thought, he still saw her as young? She'd been younger yet when she'd broached the den of several world-weary cutthroat pearl dealers in New York City, and they'd been amused, too—until they'd seen her pearls. Respect had to be earned; she appreciated that. Her tone turned crisp.

"I've also been concerned about the terms we discussed. The first pearls were to be yours, Nick, and after that we talked about an equal profit-sharing partnership." She hesitated. At the time, she'd set those terms and he'd agreed without a qualm. Since then, her own nerve in making that deal had embarrassed her—the terms had never been fair to him.

Now she found herself in the same awkward position as a kitten telling a tiger how to lap milk. Nick was a successful man, and an international importer didn't suffer fools. How could she possibly—tactfully—accuse the tiger of naiveté? "What I'm trying to say is that I know we shook hands on that agreement, but I want you to know I won't hold you to it. I think you should have the right to rethink it, once you've seen the pearls. It isn't as if we signed a legal contract."

Without any effort on her part, she seemed to have won another smile from him, perhaps in response to the scolding tone in her voice. Well, darnit, the scold was warranted. A handshake could be legally binding, but she'd urged a more formal legal contract from the beginning, not for her sake but for his. Any other pearl grower with a lick of sense would have taken Nick's formula, had it analyzed and stolen him blind. He didn't seem to care.

"It's still bothering you I wouldn't agree to that legal contract you pressed for," he said gently.

"It should be bothering *you*."

He shook his head. "From the very beginning, we were both safer with nothing on paper, and no lawyers or outsiders involved. Besides, I told you three years ago that my interest in this project has nothing to do with money. I'm only here to pay a moral debt to a man who mattered a great deal to me. Loving my grandfather, though, never meant that I believed his nutrient would work. You haven't been counting on this being your ship coming in?"

"No, of course not."

She felt the sweep of his gaze on her mouth, her throat, her eyes. "Could you relax then? I'm not going to criticize anything you've done."

"I *am* relaxed." She'd just been . . . pacing a little. She stopped abruptly and let her hands sink into the cool pockets of her silk skirt. She'd known for three years how she wanted to approach this meeting—

businesslike and honestly, informally easy but carefully impersonal. That shouldn't have been hard. Nick Langg was still essentially a stranger, and she worked with men all the time.

Only she seemed to have forgotten one small, odd detail in that scenario. Strangers didn't have three years of shared secrets between them. Strangers never had to lay trust on the line before they ever had the chance to know each other.

She'd never been able to fathom how or why he'd so readily entrusted his formula to her. The dominant character lines of his face, the hard line of his mouth, the almost bitter pride that never quite left his expression—so much about Nick implied loner. He wasn't a soft man or a dreamer. He showed no emotions or vulnerability. And it took sophistication and shrewdness to successfully compete in an international marketplace. Yet he'd trusted a woman he'd never met before with a formula that could have incomparable value.

She'd guarded that trust of his as fiercely as a she-lion did a cub, and that now lay between them, too. Dusk filtered through the tall windows, the hush of early evening. Darkness and secrets shared by two? She felt the roar of fear pounding in her ears. She'd let him in—for the pearls. Not to feel foolish female expectations because a man's eyes rested on her with curiosity, interest, gentleness.

"We need to talk about the harvest," she said abruptly.

He nodded. "I rented a house on Blue Creek. A month's lease. I hope that's adequate time."

"You won't need to be here a full month. Two weeks is more than enough time, but actually that depends on you, on the nature of the hours you want to schedule for this."

"How so?"

"Your privacy is the issue," she said simply. "Up until this point, neither my foreman, Sam, or any of my crew know anything about your project. That's how you wanted it. We can work by day or night, your choice. By day, though, my crew will definitely be around. I trust them and I absolutely trust Sam, but if you're determined to keep this completely secret—"

"Yes."

"So we work at night." She motioned helplessly with her hands. "I know you didn't want to be involved in the harvest, and I can't blame you. We're talking mosquitoes and fish smells and hours of being wet. Even the technique of opening the mussels—you can't possibly be familiar with it and there's no need for you to be. I want you to understand that I'll do the work myself, but I think it's essential that you be there, to see, to have no doubts at all about what's happened with your pearls—"

"I understand," he said wryly. "You want me to be there, just in case you suddenly fly into a fit of greed and hide the cache of pearls the minute you see them." He shook his head. "You seem to feel this need to protect me, Laura. Sometime I'll tell you exactly what a treat that is, but in the meanwhile..." He straightened from his leaning position against the desk. "Don't let a suit and starched shirt mislead you. I'll be

there, and I'll do my share of work and then some.
That's what I'm here for, not because I'm worried
about you stealing me blind. You may be stuck with a
rookie, but I swear I'm capable of learning. Will that
help?''

"Nick..." She'd never meant to offend—or
amuse—him.

"Set a time and a place." He spoke quietly, but the
order was unmistakable.

She moved swiftly for the door. "Tomorrow...at
eleven. Sometimes we work late, but everyone's always gone by that time of night. Past the lab, there's
a small brown bungalow where Sam lives. If you'll
park a little way down the road..."

"Fine."

Their business was done, yet he hesitated at the
door. They were standing less than two feet from each
other, and the tension between them suddenly crackled and spit like the flare of flame to dry tinder. Laura
promised herself that the reaction was only the pearls.
In days, even hours now, they would know. She could
stop dreaming impossible dreams, stop wanting, stop
hoping.

Except that pearls couldn't explain the odd thready
beat of her heart. Nick's lazy smiles were suddenly
gone. As if distracted before, he lavished his full attention now on her figure—the drape of silk on her
breasts, the throat hidden from his eyes, the slim long
legs too bare under her skirt. His gaze shifted. She felt
the caress of fathomless eyes on her dark hair, her
mouth, the fragile bones of her face. He'd looked be-

fore, but not like this. Yes, I see you as a woman, Laura. Did you think I was blind?

Yes, she thought fleetingly. That was exactly what she'd hoped. Exactly what she'd talked herself into believing.

"Tomorrow at eleven," he affirmed.

"Yes."

She woke up cold and trembling in the middle of the night. Silvery moonlight drifted through her open windows in a silken haze, and a soothing breeze fluttered the pale pink curtains. Dread slowly faded when her heart stopped pounding.

Sometimes months now passed before she re-dreamed the fire. Like a punishment after a stretch of peace, the dream tonight had been particularly vivid. At nineteen, she'd awakened in the dead of night to cries and smoke and flames. A wall of fire had separated her from her parents. She'd never stopped to think, but if she had, she would have made the same choices. Over the scream of fire trucks in the distance, she'd climbed onto the wrought iron balcony between the bedrooms. She could still hear the sirens, still feel the explosion of heat, the terror. Trying to drag her mother to the window, and her dad . . . dear God, her father . . .

Laura squeezed her eyes shut, forcing the memories away. Downstairs, she heard the grandfather clock chime three times. She turned her pillow to the cool side and soothed the tangled sheets.

She'd awakened from that fire in a hospital room. Such unbelievable pain—grief for her parents, the raw flame of burns on her flesh. At the time, for a long time, she'd never worried about scars. Who cared? Living was painful, and there was a home she had to find the strength to fight for, work to be done, bills to be paid. Creditors had waited, patient and kind. She'd known the townspeople all her life.

She'd also known Trevor all her life. He'd helped her paint the walls of the house. He'd sat out on the creaking swing on the front porch for hours and listened to her talk pearls. They'd picnicked by the river a dozen times. She'd taken her time, partly because she was too conscious of desperately needing him—or someone, anyone—to fill that awesome loneliness.

Of course, she was sensitive about her scars, but at twenty she had also been naive enough to believe that the right man wouldn't care. Trevor knew she'd been burned. She trusted him, and surface beauty had never seemed important to him. She'd tried to make sure of his feelings. Sweet lingering kisses in the night and leaning back against the door because she was too weak to stand. Kisses flavored with lemonade, with tea, with good morning freshness, with late afternoon spice. Before she'd invited intimacy, she knew every flavor of Trevor's kisses and she knew his touch through the increasingly annoying boundary of clothes.

She had no hesitations about giving him her virginity. She wanted that final seal of passion and love as much as he did. But the night it should have happened it simply didn't. She could still remember the look on his face when he'd slid off her blouse.

He'd tried. He couldn't make himself touch her, much less make himself even look after that first moment. He'd given her a long careful speech about getting used to it, that she couldn't doubt he loved her, that his reaction to the scars was just from such an initial shock.

It was a shock she intended to give no one else. She'd severed the relationship with Trevor. He was married now, with one son and another child on the way—to someone who wasn't flawed. She no longer missed him, and the scars she covered in silk by day had become momentum to seek perfection somewhere, anywhere else.

Flawed pearls went on a scrap pile, rejected, unwanted, unneeded by anyone. Laura drew strength from beauty, from perfection and order, from her pride. She was no one's flawed pearl.

Long into the night, she relived Nick's black eyes, the lazy sensual way he'd looked at her. Wanting was so easy, she thought fleetingly.

And she wanted, with a desperation and yearning that gnawed inside her, sharp and fierce. She wanted, but not the man. Just his pearls.

Only his pearls.

Chapter 2

The rented Mercedes died when Nick turned the key. His watch read ten-forty-five; he was early. He covered the flick of gold on his wrist with the sleeve of his sweatshirt and climbed out of the car.

A tangled thicket stretched beyond the roadside brush on his right, and to his left was Laura's property. A stand of woods—old white oaks and hardwoods and an occasional tall sycamore—marked her land. Barely a whisper of wind intruded on the peaceful stillness and the total privacy of a sultry black night. Leaning back against the car, he waited, wearing dusty boots, dark jeans and a black sweatshirt—a choice of clothes that humorously struck him as ideal attire for a thief.

With the first crackle of a leaf, every muscle in his body tightened. For an instant there was nothing to see in the darkness, just an illusion of movement and the fantasy of a woman's unique perfume. Gradually, a hundred yards distant, black took shape on black.

By now he expected her to wear a silk blouse. This one was witch-black and nestled typically just under her chin. The blouse was tucked into the waistband of dark jeans, and worn leather boots molded to her calves. Her hair had a sheen by moonlight; somehow she'd pushed it all on top of her head. A silver buckle gleamed at her waist as her hips rocked in a uniquely feminine stride. He saw the shadow of high firm breasts. He saw a magnolia-white nose and skin softer than a pearl. He saw eyes so iridescent they could have stepped out of a man's imagination.

He stood, waiting. His dreams the night before had been moody and erotic because of her. He'd awakened touchy and restless, both traits uncharacteristic of him. Because of her.

Experience had taught Nick caution with women. His heritage had taught him caution with life. If his looks were primarily American, he never forgot that he was a quarter Japanese. His American mother had died when he was young, and he'd spent most of his teenage years in Japan. By the time he was grown, he'd learned to walk the tightrope between cultures. He knew what it was to be needed but never quite trusted, wanted but never part of. He'd accepted a long time ago that there was no one else on his road.

His import business had started in the post-Vietnam era. Cambodian jade was a fast way to make a fortune for a man crazy enough to risk life and limb in a war-torn country. By twenty-six, he'd made that fortune and discovered one of those self-evident truths

that transcend continents and cultures. With enough
wealth, a man didn't have to belong anywhere.

He regularly traveled between two apartments, each
of which was filled with treasures, neither of which
was a home. Roots never took with Nick. Restlessness and loneliness were too well ingrained. He never
wasted time on the whimsical or impossible, and no
one but his grandfather, Heroshi, could have motivated him to make this nuisance trek to the Tennessee
River Valley.

If the drive for power and profit filled the empty
corners of his life, his grandfather was the only man
who ever stood between Nick and loneliness. Three
years ago, the old man had been dying when he'd
handed Nick his dream in the form of the pearl nutrient formula. There wasn't a chance it could work,
or a chance Nick would have denied Heroshi anything. To simply know would have satisfied his
grandfather. To pay the emotional debt would satisfy
Nick, and in the meantime he had no time or interest
in involving himself with a woman.

Only Laura was proving a damn good woman to
rock a man's noble intentions all to hell.

Every instinct told him that life had handed her a
blow, somewhere, sometime, but she was no one's
wounded kitten. He'd laid eyes on her and wanted her.
She wore pride as enticingly as some women wore
black satin. She had both poise and innocence, and
when the conversation turned to pearls she glowed
with the capacity for passion that was clearly part of
her. Her husky drawl was magical and she had a rare

smile that could make a man's blood burn. She didn't seem to know that.

From twenty yards away, she closed the distance between them. Silver touched her face, then shadow. He wondered, not for the first time, who her dragons were.

"You're early, Nick. I didn't think it was quite eleven yet."

"It isn't." The hint of Tennessee drawl in her voice was the hint of spice. It did something completely unnecessary to his pulse rate. "I came early, but I expected to have to wait."

He watched her hesitate. Each time she saw him she seemed to have to rejudge, remeasure, redefine some level of threat he represented to her. It was as if she had to decide each time whether she could handle him.

He could have told her she couldn't but that it hardly mattered. A man could cutthroat his way through life in the name of survival, but he didn't trample a fragile rose carelessly.

Her decision this night seemed to be made. "We both look like we're ready to rob a bank," she said demurely, motioning to their matching dark attire.

"I only wish I was that awake." That earned a soft throaty laugh—the first time he'd heard her laughter.

"I'm not in the habit of starting work this late myself." She pushed her palms down the sides of her jeans, as if they were slightly damp from nerves. "We've both been waiting for this for a long time. I can't decide if I'm more excited or more scared."

"I know the feeling." He didn't, but he took his cue from her determinedly blithe tone. "You ready to put me to work?"

"Yes, although we'll have to drive first." She gave his car a sympathetic glance. "A battered old pickup would suit us better, but it's a good two mile walk otherwise."

"No problem."

There was no road where she directed him to drive. Branches scraped the fine finish of his rental car and he didn't want to know what a scrub field could do to the Mercedes' underside. When she finally motioned him to stop, he climbed out of the car to an assault of noise—hissing insects, rustling animals sounds, the eerie snap of branches in a pitch darkness.

He was a hell of a long way from the urban environments of Tokyo and San Francisco.

"I'm afraid we're talking swamp," she told him. Her face raised to his in the moonlight. He read honesty, tension and a certain frustration in her eyes. "Normally I raise and breed my mussels in three inlets off the main river. I know those waters like I know the back of my hand, but obviously I had to choose a more private location for your experiment. None of my people ever go near the swamp."

"It's fine." Sometime soon, she was going to figure out that he wasn't going to question the decisions she'd made. "Was the land in your family a long time?" he asked.

"Since before the Civil War. Heaven knew why they held on to the swampland that long. It was never worth a Confederate penny—but then, I can't criticize much. I've had some tough financial going, but I never got around to putting this block up for sale, either. It's part of the original Jakway land; I could never seem to make myself part with it."

He'd never settled anywhere long enough to feel possessive about a piece of land, and he would have pursued it with her but there wasn't time. They neared the swamp shore. She must have arranged for the flat-bottomed boat that was moored to a stake, and once he was settled in, she used the paddle like a pole to push off through the shallow waters.

Moss blended with moonlight. Eerie sounds rippled through a sweet smelling mist and he'd never smelled smells like that in his life. They were ripe, alive, too sweet and thick, a blend of rich decaying earth and water like ink. He liked none of it.

He liked even less the thought of her setting this up alone. He hadn't fathomed the difficulties he might have brought her in simply handing over the nutrient. He wanted to take over the work and didn't know how to begin. Laura, on her knees, looked as fragile as a white rose against the harsh predator night. The swamp could have starred in a horror movie. "I'll paddle if you'll tell me where to go," he told her.

She smiled and shook her head. "I don't mind, and at this time of night it will be hard enough to spot our landing point. Just keep your hands in the boat."

He didn't ask why. He didn't want to know. "You're not normally involved in this part of the business, are you? I mean the physical work."

She chuckled. "Did you think I sat behind a desk and sifted through jewelry cases of pearls all day? This is what I do. Growing pearls is no job for a sissy and besides, I was never very good at sitting on back porches sipping lemonade.''

"So you were a tomboy?'' He didn't believe it.

"Second base, Little League. The only girl.''

He leaned back, considering that. A creature plopped in the water near them. The mist rippled through the swamp like a ghost of a ribbon. He could believe she was a white witch, a princess, a Lorelei, but there was no way in hell he could picture her at age ten, flat chested and playing second base.

Laura could feel his appraisal like the caress of a physical touch and felt a disturbing tug in her stomach. Annoyance swept through her and a tagalong exasperation. Of course, she'd already faced exactly the nature of danger Nick represented to her. To be looked at as a woman, to feel that forbidden rippling of sexual lightning clear to her toes—she wanted the feeling, she missed it, she even accepted that she needed it. She was also determined to ignore it.

They were going to spend time alone together for the next couple of weeks. It only made sense to adopt a casually friendly attitude toward Nick. They would share pearls, nothing more. Because this was her world, where she had all the controls, she had every confidence that she could control the play of the cards.

Confidence had come easily that morning, when Nick was nowhere near her. Now, rather unfortunately, he struck her as the last man a sane woman would gamble with. He looked like a warrior in the moonlight. His austere features had a hard cast and the shoulder muscles beneath his sweatshirt were rigid, as if prepared to spring into action at the first hint of trouble. His chest was like a hard wall. She could easily picture him fighting battles.

Easier yet, she could picture him in a woman's bed. It wasn't the contained power or dominant strength that would seduce a woman, but the dangerous capacity for gentleness in his eyes. Every time he looked at her, she felt those fathomless dark eyes soften. Those eyes made her feel fragile as a moonbeam. Those eyes were on her now.

She dipped the paddle and pulled, slicing through the water without making a sound. Her gaze darted to all the dark corners of the night, everywhere but on him. Casual? How was she supposed to maintain a casual friendliness when a simple look from him made it feel as if melted honey was flowing through her veins?

Pearls had to be the answer. Belatedly it occurred to her that for the first time in forever, she didn't have to control her craving to talk about pearls. "Nick?" Since his eyes hadn't left her face, it didn't take much to gain his attention. "Don't think I'm going to pry into your personal life, but you mentioned you had a grandfather, and that it was his interest in pearls that brought you here?"

"My grandfather was Japanese. For generations his side of the family grew saltwater pearls."

"But not recently?"

"No. In his younger days, he was a pearl diver—he was hurt, went on to other occupations. His interest in pearls became a more private thing after that, more a hobby, something he studied rather than being directly involved in.''

"And how did he come by this nutrient formula?"

A small smile played over his lips. For a lady who wasn't going to pry, she was doing a good job of it. "I haven't any idea," he said shortly.

"I thought . . . you might be part Japanese." She dipped and pulled, dipped and pulled, a frown pleating her forehead. "If your grandfather cared about pearls, perhaps it's just as well he wasn't directly involved in the recent past. For so many years, Japan's pearls were the best. Except for a strain of Tahitian blacks, no one was even competition for them."

"No?"

"Then they started using dyes. The economic issues were complicated—an increased market for pearls, an inability to speed production, price affected by color. Bleaches weaken the pearls, affect their long-term life, their quality." For a moment she stopped paddling. "I understand the economic crisis Japan was facing, but what they've done with their pearls is awful."

Nick had considered taking offense the minute she started talking. People had isolated him all his life for that drop of different blood. A long time ago he'd run out of patience and tolerance for other people's prejudices, but Laura was clearly coming from another place. "You and my grandfather would have definitely talked the same language," he murmured dryly. "Pearls were more sacred to him than food and shelter."

"But not to you?"

"Nothing's that sacred to me."

Except a promise to an old man, Laura thought fleetingly. The word honor crossed her mind, a word as ingrained in her Southern heritage as it was dated and old-fashioned these days. "I meant no offense when I was talking about Japan," she said softly.

"I never thought you did."

"The American market would never have come into its own if Japan hadn't run into economic troubles. It's just ... I would have wished it could have happened a different way. For their sakes, and for ours. Someone would have discovered that the valley was capable of producing better than pearl buttons or dime store necklaces anyway."

"The necklace I saw of yours in New York was a long way from a dime store necklace."

"Yes."

Something in her eyes both softened and brightened. His instincts told him that she would recognize every pearl in that necklace fifty years from now, each like a lover she could never forget. That train of thought led him to the interesting question of whether she'd ever had a lover.

"I'd adore seeing Japan," she said idly. "See the waters where they dive for the pearls. Have the chance to talk to someone about the difference between saltwater and freshwater pearls, share techniques and ideas and growing concepts...."

"That might be dangerous," Nick said smoothly.

"Dangerous. Why?"

"For the pearl grower, not for you, honey. I have the definite feeling you'd light into some unsuspecting Japanese pearl grower good and sound if you didn't like the way he handled his pearls.''

She heard nothing after the "honey." Probably it was the most common endearment that existed. Men married sixty years used it on their wives. Mattie used the word in place of names, irrespective of male or female, and Laura had used it herself on the fourteen-year-old who occasionally helped her wash windows in autumn. Endearments like that meant nothing more than the most casual of affection.

Only he said it like warm butter. And her insides felt disturbingly toasted.

She suddenly didn't want to be alone with him. Maybe she couldn't have guessed what effect moonlight and moss, heat and black satin water would have on her. Beneath her blouse, her heart beat under scars she couldn't forget. Those scars had isolated her in loneliness from intimacy for so long.

It seemed so little, to need a simple endearment. The spell of the swamp lured her into believing that's all it was. Nick looked at her, and she was terribly afraid it was more.

She dipped and pulled, watching him.

He leaned back, watching her.

He considered taking the paddle from her hands and throwing it down. He thought about what her lips would feel like crushed under his, how little it would take for a man who valued honor and control to turn primitive.

He didn't know what he'd said to make her hide behind that quiet shell again, but it couldn't have been much. She was far too sensitive. He felt like shouting that he wasn't going to hurt her. Except he couldn't be sure about that because he was beginning to want her like an obsession.

Laura mulled over the idea of turning completely around and heading home. She wanted to tell him to turn off that glow in his eyes and please leave her alone. She wasn't afraid, not of anyone, and neither fear nor distrust would necessarily have stopped her from involvement with a man. Pity was the barrier, one she'd never see in another man's eyes as long as she lived. There was no crossing that river. The bridge was permanently down.

Her chin lifted.

So did his.

And abruptly, all tension dissipated as Laura caught sight of the narrow inlet that was her landmark. She had to back paddle rapidly to angle through the bottleneck passage. Beyond were mirror-calm waters, and the bobbing cages loomed just ahead of them. The mussels' cages were suspended on long rectangular rafts that looked something like screen doors laid in the water. Excitement gleamed in her eyes. Her whole body shivered with it. Suddenly, nothing mattered but the pearls.

"You're going to need gloves," she told Nick briskly, and handed him one of two pairs from the bottom of the boat.

Nick didn't know what he'd expected, but it wasn't the messy, heavy job that followed. The mussels were swaddled in nets, and six net cages were suspended from each raft. The nets were immersed in shallow waters no more than two or three meters deep. Laura had peeled off her leather boots and slid off the boat to stand in that muck bottom before he could stop her. She hauled in the first heavy length of net before he'd even leaned over the side of the boat.

"Let me do that."

"I know what I'm doing, Nick. You'll just get in the way."

"Dammit, woman." She had a way of cutting a man's ego down to size.

"I'm serious. I didn't want you here for the work, but so you could see what I was doing, so you could know how your pearls were being handled. Just let me do it all."

He paid no attention, peeling off his boots and dropping down beside her in the water. The gritty bottom sucked at his feet, cold and slimy.

"Now we'll both have wet feet, for no reason at all," she scolded. "Just get back in the boat."

She obviously had no intention of telling him what to do, so he watched and mimicked what she did. The long nets were dripping mud; she handled each like it was china. The creatures inside were hardly aromatic, and the job wouldn't have been so heavy if the nets hadn't been tangled in everything from sand and muck to weeds. His lady of the magnolia skin and haunting blue eyes didn't seem to notice the mess. Her laughter burst free and natural and she obviously had a love for the hopelessly ugly mussels. "Aren't they beautiful?"

"Breathtaking," he concurred gravely. "How many more?"

She climbed nimbly back in the flat-bottomed boat. "Just this for tonight. We can only handle so many at a time. My workers will be around the lab by nine in the morning. We'll have our hands full to tackle this many by then—getting them back to the lab, extracting the pearls and having everything cleaned up." She glanced at him. "You didn't do too bad for a rookie."

"You're the one who did all the work."

"You'll have your chance." She handed him the paddle. "About a half mile west the swamp thins out. We edge around a little peninsula and then you'll recognize the cove and the lab. *Then* we get to carry all these nice little babies inside. Sound like fun?"

"Sounds like something I've never done at two in the morning before," Nick said, noticing that she had a smudge of dirt on her nose and her hair had come tumbling down. The entire time he rowed she never stopped fussing with the nets. Thick velvet lashes brushed her cheeks, as fragile as dew caught in a spider web. Nick felt a pull inside him like he'd never felt for a woman before. "Are you cold?"

She gave a small, startled laugh. "You have to be joking. In less than an hour, we're going to know! But we're not going to judge your formula on just this night's harvest. Don't get discouraged until we've seen all of them," she continued firmly.

"All right."

"Anything could happen to a single string of mussels. That's why I planted them in different places. These look marvelously healthy, but there's no way to know until we get near light, until we open them. I don't want you to be disappointed."

"I won't be," he assured her.

"If you don't mind my admitting it, I never really believed in your nutrient. The concept is exciting, yes. Obviously the nutrition available to the mussel has to affect the quality of pearls it's capable of producing. But it has to have been tried before, Nick. Don't count on it working."

She was counting on it, though. He saw it in the blaze of emotion in her eyes, in all the concentrated passion. Her shell was gone again. She'd forgotten to be wary. She was completely unaware that her damp silk blouse clung to her breasts, that the rippling curtain of dark hair flowed behind her in blatant sexual invitation to touch.

The promise of pearls loosened the lover in Laura, and the lover in Laura gradually unraveled the man. Nick felt a blaze of heat and the need to touch her was like a wash of magic. And he wanted to capture her laughter, savor it, memorize it.

In another arena, exhaustion was hitting him in waves by the time she finally motioned him to beach the boat in a hidden shelter of brush. Damp, chilled and muddy, he hauled the netted cages to his shoulders, his four for her two. She ducked and skirted the shadows of trees. He followed the sway of her hips. She could have been leading him to hell and he wouldn't have raised a fuss.

Her lab was as black as the night. Inside, she closed the blinds and locked the door before lighting a kerosene lantern. She set the lantern on the floor. "It will be less likely to throw shadows through the windows here. Sounds ridiculously cloak-and-dagger, doesn't it? But we've managed to keep the secret this long."

By then the floor was a mess of mud and water and nets. Oblivious, she knelt in the middle of it. So did he, watching and doing as she did to free the eight-inch mussels from their netted captivity. It touched him that her fingers were slightly trembling.

"Now, don't count on this," she reminded him.

"I'm not, Laura."

"Both of us ... we'd be terribly foolish to really count on this."

"Yes."

Six mussels were gradually freed from their netted cages, then the next six, then all of them. She sprang up, rummaged in a drawer and returned with a tool that looked something like a dentist's probe. He couldn't remember feeling more frustrated. He was at home in a Tokyo boardroom; he'd coped in a Cambodian jungle. It was his nature to take charge, not to watch a woman do the work. Still, other dynamics came into play when she raised the probe tool toward him.

"I should let you do the first one. After all, this whole project is yours."

It obviously killed her to offer. "Go ahead."

"No, really. It isn't fair."

"I haven't any idea what you're doing until I've watched you once," he reminded her.

"I could tell you." But she lifted a bumpy shelled mussel like it was her firstborn.

He sighed. "Look, just do it, would you please?"

"Well..."

She'd said her choice of mussels species was strong. He saw how strong when he realized what it took to force the shell open. Her jaw clenched in concentration and her shoulders tensed. Finally, after more than an hour of frenetic activity, she split the first shell in two and went totally still.

"Oh, God," she whispered.

Inside the shell was a murky smooth slime, so ugly that it seemed impossible that nature would have chosen such an unappealing source to nurture anything beautiful. Nestled in that unlikely bed were four black pearls.

"Oh, God," she whispered again. "They have to be ten millimeters. But there could be a flaw, Nick. On the undersides. I've got the cleaning solution ready and when we get them out, when we..."

She was impatient. So, suddenly, was Nick. Her hands held the sides of the mussel; he knew she wasn't about to drop it. For all the mess and water and confusion, he couldn't take his eyes off her mouth. He moved forward, closing the distance between them. Her face shot up, more in surprise than wariness when his hands closed on her tense shoulders.

He had to touch her. There was no choice involved. He wasn't sure if the element of choice had disappeared when she'd scolded him for being in the way, or when she'd walked to him out of that darkness at the beginning of the night. He had more on his mind than Laura and there seemed only one way to quell his irrational fascination for a woman who couldn't be less of his world.

But kissing her didn't help. Her lips were already parted when his mouth covered hers. His hands glided along her shoulders until his palms cradled her face, holding her still. So vulnerable. She knelt with her throat bared; he could see the thread of heartbeat in her pulse. She tasted warm and sweet and she was trembling. Huge blue eyes opened wide on his. *Don't*, they pleaded.

But she didn't move away. An ache started deep in his groin like a lick of fire. Her lashes shimmered down when his mouth glided on hers again, this time with the taste of pressure, the flavor of fever. He'd never expected such innocence. He hadn't kissed a woman in years who didn't know what to do with her mouth, her tongue.

His lips were firmly cradling hers when he reached down and stole the mussel shell from her hands. She didn't protest but neither did she move to touch him. She was so tense, when all he wanted to do was drench her in softness.

His fingers coiled around her waist, gently drawing her to him until the tips of her breasts brushed his chest. A little closer and those breasts molded to him. He could smell the perfume of her skin, feel the rising heat of her body. A helpless, angry whisper escaped her throat that was more vibration than sound.

Too fast, too awkwardly, her hands suddenly groped for him. Her fingers wrapped themselves in the thickness of his hair and her mouth turned hot and pliant under his. He doubted she had any idea what she was doing. He couldn't possibly have anticipated the explosion of passion unleashed from her. She twisted against him with sweet, strong urgency as if she'd never tasted desire. She was shaking with it.

He touched the white column of her throat, her nape, the fragile length of her spine. His palm ached to cup her hips, grind her closer to him, but he didn't dare. His body was already hardened in tense, coiled readiness to take her. He knew damn well she wasn't ready for that, nor was this the time and place.

He released her mouth to glide his lips along the curve of her jaw. His tongue flicked out to taste her. That bit of honey was never going to be enough.

He struggled for the control he had always taken for granted. It took longer to retrieve it than it should have. When he finally pulled back, his fingers were in her hair and this thumbs gently traced her cheekbones. Black diamonds blazed in his eyes when he unsmilingly searched her face. Her skin had a pale flush, her eyes looked shocked and she wasn't breathing at all well. He'd never felt more powerful as a man.

"I..."

He waited.

"I... perhaps it was natural we got carried away."

"Perhaps," he murmured.

"The pearls. They're so perfect, Nick."

"Yes."

"But now we have so much to do. We have to hurry."

"Yes."

"I don't want you to think... I mean, it was just the moment. I'm sure you feel that way, too. Seeing the pearls. *Anyone*, seeing pearls like these..."

"Yes." For the moment, she could have said the sky was orange and he would have agreed. Right now he was willing to let her believe anything she wanted to believe.

He knew, which she clearly didn't, that there would be another time.

Chapter 3

It wouldn't happen again. Laura closed her eyes, feeling the river breeze tangle her hair in humid mist.

She had honest answers for the night before. The kiss wasn't just the result of the blind exhilaration that had welled up in her when she'd seen the pearls. It was more than that. Responsibilities and worries had dominated her life for as long as she could remember. A woman could get tired of fighting. A woman sometimes needed to believe that she wasn't alone.

To make something more than that from a spontaneous embrace would be foolish. Another woman—a normal woman—wouldn't. And exactly because scars separated her from other women, Laura knew it wouldn't happen again.

The tiller suddenly vibrated beneath her hands. She quickly opened her eyes and images of Nick and black pearls immediately disappeared. She'd nearly missed the turn. Groaning loudly, the brailer chopped through the current toward shore.

On its best days, the boat looked like a gypsy wagon on the water. Its battered stern was scarred with dents. Hanging nets fluttered seaweed in the wind, and its engine coughed and groaned for every river swell. Brailers used to be the main river craft used by fresh-water pearlers, but that was decades ago. Every year Laura claimed she was going to sink the old devil. She never did. The old craft might be troublesome and cranky, but it could carry an elephant and still stay afloat.

Elephants weren't her cargo this morning, but nets of Pigtoe mussels being hauled in for harvest. Sam was on a parts run in town, and the four man crew she'd taken with her looked as disreputable as their craft.

Before the rope was tied to the dock, Abe and George were up and moving toward the work yard by the lab. Neither had wasted a spare word over the last four hours, and Tom was equally taciturn. Although their sullen silence could have been a product of the unbearable humid heat, or a morning working in mud shallows over the sing of mosquitoes, Laura knew well that that wasn't the cause of their silence.

Her eyes trained on the last member of their mini-crew. Simon Howard had only been on the payroll for five days. In contrast to the others, he knew how to use a razor, hadn't once shown up with beer breath, and his clean-cut looks were a wonderful difference from the derelicts who usually looked for river work.

Impossible tiredness flooded her in those few seconds while she waited for Abe, George and then Tom to walk out of hearing range. She hadn't slept at all the night before. Her canvas shoes were damp, her blouse and jeans were clinging to her, and her pinned-up hair felt like ten pounds of heat and weight.

When her fourth crew member had a booted foot on the stern, her voice turned brisk, full of all that energy she didn't have. "Simon?" He turned back to look at her, his arms full of cages and his smile on the ready. "Get your gear and get off the place. You're fired," she said quietly.

His brown eyes iced over with hostility so fast that she could have kicked herself for not seeing the bad-news potential of this man before hiring him. "What is this? You got some complaint about my work?"

"You can outwork Abe and Tom twice over." She reached for her share of nets and gear. "I'll make your check out at the office. Be there. I'll expect you permanently off the property within fifteen minutes."

"You ain't got no call to do that! What the hell you think I'm supposed to have done?"

She ignored him, feeling those ice eyes on her back, then his explosive "bitch" spit out loud enough to raise Abe's head in the distance. She saw Abe share looks with the rest of the crew, and walked on.

The shade of the lab wasn't any cooler than the sunbaked yard. She dropped her gear, rubbed her damp palms on her jeans and strode toward the desk. Her hands were shaking while she made out his check. Her hands always shook when she had to fire someone.

It wasn't easy finding a good work crew, men willing to work in river mud and rain and hot sun with anything as stinky as mussels. George had a record, so did Tom. She'd never cared where a man had been or why. She paid each higher wages than she could afford and she never asked anything from her crew she didn't do herself. She put up with hangovers and an occasional binge, but in return she expected loyalty. She had to have loyalty.

Simon's rigid shoulders suddenly blocked the doorway, his eyes glittering rage. "I never took nothing."

"No? Step foot on the property again and I'll call the police," she said calmly.

"What the hell are those few lousy pearls to you? Don't think I'll forget this. You better be looking over your shoulder."

She could have told him that a few lousy pearls really were nothing to her. The harvest of Three-Ridge mussels the day before was never going to reap a heavy profit. Quality had been disappointing... almost as disappointing as watching Simon sneaking the booty into his jeans pockets. He'd made his second mistake in flaunting his loot in front of the others that morning.

She watched his broad back as he stormed toward his car. When he gunned the engine, she could see the glare of his face through the streaked car windshield. Was it contorted with hate, rage? The look was ugly and distressing enough to make her stomach turn over. She looked back and forth at Abe, George and Tom, crowded in the shade with their lunch buckets, suddenly talking a mile a minute about the weather and the work and fishing.

She wasted one wry minute mentally damning all men in general, then straightened her shoulders. None of her crew would have snitched on a fellow worker, but none of them wanted a thief in their midst, either. Those that had played tag with the law knew exactly what they had—maybe their last and only chance for an honest job at a decent wage. She'd seen them stick by her through good harvests and bad. They expected *her* to find the viper in the pack, though, weed him out on her own and handle herself—when it came down to it—like a man.

She did, she had, and she would. Some days, though, she felt...scared. Small. Annoyingly female.

For the dozenth time that morning, Nick's image drifted in her mind, and before she could banish it her eyes wandered to the tiled floor under her desk. No hinge or handle showed on the surface, but her fireproof minivault was underneath the tile.

Inside it this morning were two handfuls of flawless, exquisite black pearls—the pearls that weren't possible, that couldn't be, the result of a formula that couldn't work. They'd barely started Nick's harvest. A dream she'd never expected to come to life was suddenly exploding possibilities in front of her eyes.

Only she'd never expected to also have emotions explode inside her when Nick touched her—tangled, bittersweet, complicated emotions. She'd never mastered being tough, but she'd long credited herself with a stronger will than any man she'd ever come across. It should have been simple, avoiding that embrace. It should have been even easier to not respond to it. She never forgot her scars. She never allowed herself illusions about what she couldn't have.

The telephone next to her jangled, and fantasies of pearls and a man faded into a grueling hot afternoon and one glitch after another. Sam returned from town, furious she'd tackled firing Simon without him, and Sam in a sulk was more than capable of being a royal pain. The Pigtoe mussels in Crader's Cove showed signs of a weakening microorganism; they had to be taken out of production. The pickup blew a tire. The crew grew more quarrelsome as clouds picked up ominous momentum in the west.

By three in the afternoon, Laura was hot, tired, and in no mood to have Sam fetch her from the lab for the interruption of yet another phone call. At the same time she snatched up the phone, she tugged open the desk drawer in the hopes of finding a forgotten candy bar or bag of nuts. It wasn't that she'd forgotten to eat lunch; there hadn't been time.

"Miss Jakway? Nat Hemming here."

She pushed the drawer closed with a snap, forgetting hunger. "Mr. Hemming!" she interjected with an amazing amount of cordial surprise. "What can I do for you?"

"Been trying to get ahold of you for two weeks now. Thought you and me might sit down to lunch sometime. Should have gotten together a long time ago. Seems to me we have a lot in common, now that you've got yourself involved in some fancy breeding techniques these days."

There was a moment's pause while she waited for her heart to climb back down from her throat. At least she finally had a reason for Hemming's phone calls, and she'd guessed that her neighbor knew she was experimenting with more than dime store pearls. "I can't imagine anything I could ever do that a pearl grower of your size could be interested in," she said pleasantly.

"I'm sure that's true, but I like to help a neighbor."

"How kind of you." She kept the wry note from her voice only with an effort. Hemming maintained a pillar of the community image in Silverwater. Every time he set out to help a neighbor, though, the property inevitably ended up with his name on it in a matter of months. "Your lunch idea sounds delightful, but unfortunately, my schedule's rather full—"

"You got a mortgage payment due in sixty days, I understand." Hemming's Tennessee twang was as lethal as a sweet mint julep. "As an officer at the bank, I consider it my business to keep tabs on local industries. Can't tell when anyone's going to need a little help in this economy. Wednesday at noon suit you? My place."

It didn't suit her at all, but she agreed. Meeting him was a sound business choice, she told herself when she hung up the phone. This harvest was proving a little nip and tuck in terms of profit, but she hoped for yield from her private work as well, and for three years she'd been meeting her bank payments on time. Hemming represented no threat to her. What if he did know that she'd had a few special successes with breeding techniques? What could he do? Nothing. Why should he even care?

Absently she rubbed her temple with two fingers, and then straightened. She'd find out at lunch whether Hemming intended to be friend or enemy. Either way she'd handle him. No one was going to take away everything she'd built so hard to keep.

Still, when she pushed open the lab door and headed back to the work yard, her nerves were edging toward frayed. Between a sleepless night, firing a man, the argument with Sam, no lunch and Nat Hemming, anybody could explain a slight problem with irritability.

Only those weren't the real reasons her nerves were jangling. The daylight hours kept passing with relentless speed. She couldn't get Nick off her mind and she didn't want to face him again.

Taking risks took courage, which she had plenty of. It also took judgment, the pride to keep going when the odds were against you, the strength to do what you had to do. Sometimes it meant putting everything you had and everything you were on the line. Laura had taken risks at every one of those levels and never looked back. Pearls were worth it.

For the first time since she was nineteen, though, she faced the only price for pearls that she was not willing to pay.

Nick had made her feel fragile. Shatterable. Vulnerable as a woman.

It couldn't happen again.

Bunched clouds hid the crescent moon from view, and Nick could smell rain in the wind. The hot night breeze rustled through leaves like the crinkle of a woman's taffeta petticoat, all tease and promise, no relief. The barometer was falling, and every leaf and blade of grass knew it. The pressure of waiting and anticipation had Nick pacing until Laura stepped out of the darkness. He took one look at her face and mentally cursed.

She was dressed in brown cotton pants and a matching plain blouse with a mandarin collar. She'd pinned up her hair schoolmarm style, an effect that was undoubtedly supposed to be cool and severe, and instead relentlessly accented her princess-perfect bones and pure skin. Fragile. The word had haunted him the night before, but she raised another emotion in him now. Simple fury.

It had never occurred to him that she'd be fool enough to work last night and then all day, then turn around and expect to put in another working night with him. The hollows shadowing her eyes said it all.

"I hope you haven't been waiting? I thought I was early."

"You were," Nick agreed. She barely glanced at him when she slid into the passenger side of the Mercedes. "Do you want me to drive to the same place?"

"Yes. You remember where to go?"

"No problem." The engine purred to life; he pushed the lights on low. "We'll have to set up something different after this," he said casually.

"Something different?"

"Different hours, to accommodate whatever work schedule you have during the day."

"There's no need for that. I know you don't want to be in the area any longer than you have to be, and this experimental harvest of yours won't take that long if we simply get to it. In fact . . ." She hesitated. "At first I was sure we were talking two to three weeks, but I believe we can work much faster than that."

If she killed herself working double shifts? "Good," he murmured. "Same boat, same area in the swamp tonight?"

She shook her head. "We're headed to a completely different bend in the river."

He could tell that from the cool frost in her voice, but she was talking about pearls not their fragile relationship. He noted the hands folded politely in her lap, the ankles delicately crossed, the stiff posture. She could make brown denim look like elegant attire, but those soft eyes of hers were glazed with exhaustion. She was so busy being Strong with a capital S that she didn't notice his sack until the car was stopped and he threaded the canvas pack on his back.

"Something for later," he answered her unspoken question. Just like the night before, the flat-bottomed boat was waiting for them, and again she grabbed and untied the mooring ropes before he could help her.

The shadows were black in the silent night. An uneasy stillness and a feeling of isolation and pending storm pervaded the swamp. He could barely see twenty feet ahead of them, and for the first leg of the ride, he didn't talk, didn't try and didn't offer to take the oars. When a woman was on a crash course with determination, a man was wise to let be. He wondered vaguely if she was more upset because he'd made the pass last night or because she'd responded to it.

Her dowdy brown didn't work, of course, any more than the hairpins or the brisk frostiness of her voice. That she even tried such unsophisticated techniques told Nick how little she knew of men. He mentally corrected the thought as fast as it surfaced. It was possible she knew her share of men. Just not predators. There was a vast difference, and all day he'd felt the drag of that conscience. Leave her alone, Langg, he warned himself.

He wanted to. The swamp gradually enfolded them in mist and stillness. He found a comfortable position on the splintery seat, wanting to keep his eyes off her, unable to. She poled off from shore and paddled at a faster rate than the night before. Sleek and swift, the oars dipped in the water. Every pull showed the strain on her features. Her lips compressed with the energy she was demanding of herself. She was in a fine mood to take on an army single-handed.

She was also so close to collapse she couldn't see straight. It took her twenty minutes before she proved that there was an ounce of common sense in that sweet stubborn head of hers. "Last night you offered to row." Her tone was humorously wry, certainly not complaining.

"I would have offered tonight, but it was obvious you know your way around here so well. Are you tired?"

"Not at all."

"I didn't think so, but I'll take a turn with the paddles if you're bored."

"I'm not bored. I just . . ."

She was so damn tired she didn't know what she was. He pushed his sack in front of her at the same time he smoothly took the oars. "Open it," he suggested.

Even by nine that night, Laura had been certain she could handle Nick and the night ahead. The cramping exhaustion from a sleepless night and a rotten day had disappeared. Her body had taken the punishment of long hours before, and her second wind—third wind? fourth wind?—had taken the form of an odd, reckless energy. She'd tried to nap earlier in the evening but it was useless. She'd never been able to sleep on a problem.

True, Nick wasn't a problem. And as soon as she proved that to herself—whether or not they harvested a single pearl this night—maybe that taut, achy, annoying jumpiness inside her would ease.

The contents of his knapsack immediately changed her mood, but that was more like exchanging one cliff edge for another.

"Careful," he warned.

She was very careful with the two slim-stemmed glasses, the dripping cold, packed bottle of champagne. She looked at him.

"There's something else in there."

With criminal negligence he'd packed a rose in his canvas sack. Just one, its thorns removed, its color an impossibly delicate peach. The bud hadn't opened yet. Petals layered satin on satin, pure and perfect. An unflawed beauty, Laura thought, and felt an overwhelming rush of helplessness. The gaze she fastened on Nick was vulnerable, angry, soft. "I don't know what to say."

"There isn't anything to say. Yesterday's pearls obviously required some kind of celebration."

"Is that a Nick Langg rule?" she asked wryly.

"That's a Nick Langg rule," he affirmed. "Can you manage the bottle?"

She shook her head. "Nick, really, this is completely unnecessary. And very honestly, I never drink."

"I'm afraid it's completely necessary. Not for you or me, but for my grandfather. I don't give a hoot in hell what we come up with tonight or from now on. Surely you're aware that what we found last night alone is worth a small fortune?"

"Those pearls haven't been appraised," she reminded him.

"And I wouldn't know what they were worth from Adam. But you do, Laura, and last night I saw in your eyes what you thought of their value. Open the bottle."

"I—"

"This is for my grandfather," he repeated. "You can't possibly refuse to toast my grandfather."

Her lips parted, and then closed. He watched her work at the metal fastener covering the cork and mentally asked Heroshi's forgiveness. Heroshi would never have approved using tricks to wile a woman, would have accepted no excuses for a predator closing in on an innocent.

But his grandfather couldn't see Laura, the sensual promise in her eyes, the skin softer than cream, the way she held that rose as if she were afraid someone was going to take it away from her.

The cork popped high and loud. The fat plop in the black water in the distance momentarily stilled the frogs. Her smile made him smile.

He pushed the oars in the boat when he understood she was only going to pour herself a sip. He dipped the champagne bottle deep into both glasses, and the boat drifted aimlessly as crystal clicked on crystal.

"Champagne and swamps—I don't believe this," she scolded, but she obediently raised her glass to clink with his. "To your Heroshi—if I've said his name correctly?"

"You did," he agreed, and lifted the glass a second time. "Now, to our pearls."

"To our pearls," she murmured.

He had more toasts. To the Japanese pearl market. To the American pearl market. To frogs. Clouds were gathering with brooding speed overhead; he insisted they needed a toast to ward off rain. He wormed her age out of her and then toasted the general age of twenty-seven. They toasted all pearl lovers in the universe. They toasted roses.

The fine wine shimmered in her veins and she felt a helpless lassitude stealing over her. It wasn't that she'd forgotten their pearls—nothing could make her forget the pearls—any more than anything could make her put aside her responsibilities, her work, her life, her past. But laughter was such a luxury, and the spell of Nick was the spell of a moment out of time.

Such silliness wasn't real. The man dressed in panther-black with sexy dark eyes and a lazy smile

looking at her through the darkness like he'd just met
Eve must be an illusion. She wasn't Eve. She was just
a woman who'd had a really terrible day pile up on
her. And the euphoria of two glasses of champagne
coaxed her into believing there was no harm in taking
ten minutes off just to be silly. Lazy. To remember
how special it felt to just be a woman.

"Nick, we're drifting," she said finally.

"Good." His back against the stern, Nick's one leg
was propped on the splintered seat.

"If we don't get a move on soon, it's going to rain."

"We're going to get a move on, very soon, but I
think both of us needed to find something out about
each other." Slowly he shifted positions and reached
for the oars. "I have another Nick Langg rule I didn't
mention to you."

"Not another one?" she asked wryly.

"Another one," he affirmed. "People who share
champagne in a swamp have to relax together. That's
the rule. Laura?"

She motioned him to paddle toward the east fork in
the water. He could see on her face that she was fighting to return to business and cool friendliness again.
They both had to duck for a cobweb strand of moss
hanging long and low from a gnarled cypress tree.

"I'm not your enemy," he said quietly.

Her eyes jumped to his, startled. "I never thought
you were—"

"You've been uneasy around me from the first. A
certain level of wariness is a healthy dimension in most
business relationships, but that isn't quite what we
have. This isn't a competitor relationship, Laura.

We're never going to be at odds over what happens or doesn't happen with these pearls, simply because neither of us took on this project for money. Your love was for the experiment itself, and it shows up in everything you do. And I'm just a man, paying a very old-fashioned debt of honor to a grandfather I loved very much. I'm not asking you to trust me. I learned too long ago that having to ask for trust is a contradiction in terms. I'm just asking you to..." He hesitated. "To talk to me."

He pulled the dripping oars in the boat and looked at her, waiting.

"If I've done or said something to make you uncomfortable—" she started hopelessly.

"You wanted to establish a certain distance, I respect that. You barely know me, and we're only going to spend time together for the next two weeks. But then, that's the point, Laura. We're two strangers stuck with each other for a short period of time. Is there a reason we can't simply be easy with each other?"

She studied him, this man who only had to breathe to arouse a fierce ache of uneasy emotions inside of her. She suddenly saw all her careful behavior around him as immature. Nick was stuck in a Tennessee backwater town for two weeks alone, knowing no one. How could she have been so self-centered as to ignore a stranger's basic need for a little companionship? As he said, he was just a man. Not her enemy.

"No reason at all," she said lightly.

* * *

Over the next three nights, Laura discovered that he'd lied. They worked side by side in the water and darkness, sometimes becoming so exhausted they were slaphappy. Laughter made the work easier; sharing made the time pass. He never touched her, but it was never someone to talk to that Nick wanted.

He didn't know how to talk. He willingly listened when she told him about Mattie and Sam, about the Jakway history in the shell industry, but coaxing him to share experiences was like pulling teeth.

She gently pulled those teeth, certainly not because she wanted to encourage a relationship, but because Nicholas Langg was a lonely man. He wasn't at all what she first thought. He described his apartments in San Francisco and Tokyo. Neither sounded like a home. Heroshi was the only relative he ever mentioned. His work took him to endless exotic places, but the experiences he related to her spoke of restlessness, challenge, even danger—never contentment. He would have her believe that wealth and power were important to him, but she'd never met another human being who needed laughter as much as he did, a chance to just be, to release a little control. Had so many people judged Nick Langg so harshly?

She ignored the roses he brought her every night— the first coral, the second white, the third a pale, pale pink. She ignored a lot of things that she probably shouldn't have: the way he looked at her sometimes, the way his voice gentled when he was talking to her. She was being drawn into a web of feeling wanted and protected and cherished. Maybe she ignored so much because, simply, she needed to.

Pride had always been the reason she'd kept intimacy out of her relationships with men. In Nick, she found another human being who understood pride as well as she did. He'd always walked alone. So had she.

If he'd tried to make another pass, she'd never have had to trust him. But he didn't touch her. When their second cache of pearls surpassed the first in quality, she waited. Their third night together, they harvested her control mussels, the ones that had not been injected with his nutrient. She'd waited that night, too. And on the fourth night she'd been exhausted. She'd woken from a short catnap in the boat to find he'd done all the work hauling in nets. He'd had ample time to take advantage of her, but he simply didn't.

The magic of just being with him proved a growing temptation. Nick didn't know about the fire, her scars. He never would. Was it so criminally wrong to need the soft laughter in the dark nights, to share as any woman wanted to share with a man? He was so damned lonely. He made her feel impossibly rich when she managed to coax laughter out of him. He made her feel beautiful, unflawed, special, and if she built up crazy illusions over those nights—they seemed so harmless. No one would know. Nothing could happen.

But then came Wednesday, and the storm.

Chapter 4

At eleven-thirty on Wednesday morning, Laura ran up the veranda steps, dropped a soaking wet pair of work boots outside the door and passed an open-mouthed Mattie on the staircase. "I know, I know! I look like a river rat, and I have exactly twenty minutes to transform into Ms. Business. Fifty cents?"

Mattie shook her head with a chuckle. "I've told you before. I don't gamble with fast-change artists."

Twenty minutes and a short drive later, Laura's aging Datsun paused at the locked gate of the Hemming estate. Once admitted, she followed the circular drive, passing by flourishing gardens and a rolling sweep of meticulously groomed lawn. The sprawling ranch house was a contemporary beauty, with sun panels and a shadowed arbor courtyard.

She climbed out of the car with a rueful smile. Modern wasn't her style, but she valued perfection in any form. Hemming's lawn looked like a gardener had knelt at the edges with fingernail scissors for every grass blade. She tackled the three acres around her own house with a rusty forty-year-old tractor.

Determinedly she pulled her purse strap to her shoulder. Her dark hair was swept back, a paisley blouse in rose hues matched a rose linen skirt and pumps. A slim gold watch wrapped her wrist and luminous pearls with a pink hue adorned her ears. If Laura didn't have the money to overhaul the Jakway grounds the way they should be, she had the pride to expect perfection of herself. A woman measured confidence in looking her best.

Laura both looked and felt her best as she mounted the three steps to the front door. Thunderclouds had rolled in days ago from the west, but they'd just hovered, ominous and angry, refusing to spill rain. The heavy, restless atmosphere was the exact opposite of her mood. It wasn't that she thought she could conquer continents single-handed, but she had a treat in store for Mr. Hemming if he had any preconceptions about submissive or easily intimidated Southern women.

A woman in navy blue answered the door and led her through a long hallway to a patio overlooking a diamond-shaped pool. She only had glimpses of gleaming antiques and crystal and beautifully framed oils before she was outside again, settled in a white wrought iron chair with a chintz cushion. The table beside her was set with linen and china, but Nat Hemming was nowhere in sight.

"He should be here shortly, Miss."

"Fine." Laura nodded pleasantly to the woman.

She spent a bare five minutes with a fretful breeze before Nat Hemming appeared in the far doorway, a tall florid man with a mane of wonderful white hair. "Laura, you're early. I'm sorry if I kept you waiting," he said jovially.

"No problem at all." He offered a hand and she shook it. The matched pair of strong handshakes didn't take long, and then he seated himself across from her and pulled at a napkin.

"Shall we wait to talk business until after lunch?"

"Fine."

All through the meal, she wondered why she'd wasted so much anxiety worrying this meeting. Nat's smiles were cordial and his attitude paternal, even affectionate. He poured a clear white wine to match a delicious crabmeat salad and made every effort to make sure she was comfortable. Expecting a confrontation, she found nothing but a relaxed neighbor who was going out of his way to charm her.

Laura had never been easily charmed, but she was also aware that she'd perhaps unfairly prejudged Hemming on his reputation. His looks reminded her of fine wine, basic clean-cut bones that had aged to strikingly distinguished. His blue eyes were buried in crow's feet and his skin had the leathered texture of a working man. His khaki shirt was hand tailored and his slacks were meticulously creased, but they were basically work clothes. She respected that. Even his rumbling enemies gave Hemming credit for making his fortunes on his own sweat and determination. She respected that, too.

"It isn't often I share lunch with a beautiful young woman, Laura. As I said on the phone, we should have done this a long time ago."

"It was kind of you to invite me," she remarked, and added impulsively, "Your house and grounds...everything shows so much care and time, Mr. Hemming. It's really lovely."

"Why, thank you. You've probably heard from the local grapevine that I grew up in a one-room shack, scrambling for river work from the time I was ten. Coming from that background, I confess I've developed a terrible weakness for beautiful things," he admitted.

When the lady in blue slipped the lunch dishes on a tray and disappeared, Nat leaned forward and pulled a reed-thin cigar from his pocket. Nothing changed in his smile—nothing changed about anything—but Laura suddenly felt the seep of uneasiness. All he did was push the little wheel on a solid gold lighter. From nowhere there was flame and her neighbor's eyes trained on her face with shrewd intensity.

"You don't mind if I smoke, do you? I enjoy the luxury of a cigar after meals."

The flame danced between them, hovering between her hand and his, nowhere near the tip of his cigar where it should be. An odd shiver touched her deep inside, and an old relentless phobia tried to surface. It wasn't Hemming's fault that she hated fire. All fire. No pain matched the hell-sear agony of a fire burn. "Of course I don't mind," she said smoothly.

"You're sure?"

She had to take a deep breath and force her eyes away from the hypnotizing flame. "I'm sure," she said lightly.

"Fine." Finally the cigar was lit and he snapped his lighter closed. Briskly he raised two small leather cases from the chair beside him. "I brought something to show you."

She opened both cases to find single strands of pearls nestled on black velvet in each. "Orient" was a pearl man's term for luster, and both necklaces glowed with a special light and luminescence. Both were unique, although a layman would never have been able to distinguish the two in quality. Laura's eyes inevitably softened on the strand of pearls to her right.

Her neighbor chuckled. "I knew you'd recognize your own—I picked them up in New York on a trip last winter. The necklace on your left is mine. Came out of the valley four years ago."

"Exquisite," Laura said honestly, but a restless breeze suddenly feathered over her skin. Hemming had done nothing. She was trying her best to revise her judgment of him, but she had the oddest urge to pick up her pearls and fly. The instinct was simply and totally irrational: she didn't want him to have them. A thousand times she'd envisioned her pearls on a woman's bare neck where they belonged, where her pearls would have a chance to breathe and glow on a woman's skin. Not locked in this man's safe where no one could see them.

"I collect pearls as well as grow them, you know. This is the third piece of yours I've seen." His cigar had gone out, and the lighter flamed in front of her eyes again. Hemming's gaze fastened on hers, and she kept seeing his smile through the flame.

Light it. Just light it, would you please?

"You have an incredible amount to be proud of, honey."

"Thank you." That flame danced within millimeters of the linen napkin before his cigar was lit again. Laura slid her hands to her lap, too aware they'd become ice-cold. She was imagining all this of course. Imagining he was playing games with that lighter. She was imagining it because she was an extremely foolish woman with a phobia about fire that one of these days she was going to banish to Timbuktu. "Mr. Hemming, would you mind telling me how you knew those pearls were mine?" she asked quietly.

"Sweetheart, I could identify any pearls that came out of this valley with both eyes closed in a black room. I expect, so could you. I also knew Macklin—you know Macklin in Camden?"

"Not personally. I've seen his pearls."

"Yes. Well, Macklin only wished he could command a price at the level of those necklaces in front of you." Smoke billowed around his face as he leaned back, the cigar clamped between his teeth and the lighter in his right hand. He flicked it open, then closed. Laura told herself that everyone had nervous habits. Hemming's tone couldn't have been more confiding or cordial.

"Macklin's been my only competition in this valley for years. For that matter, it took me thirty years to have the know-how to produce pearls of this quality. Honey, I look at you, and you're so damned young you make me shake my head. You've either had one heck of a lot of luck or the kind of instinct some men would kill for in this business."

She touched her fingers to her forehead. Open, closed. Open. Closed. If he would just leave the lighter alone, she'd be able to concentrate, and his compliment certainly wanted to rush to her head. Her neighbor knew pearls. There were days she craved the chance to share her accomplishments with someone. Anyone. "My family were in pearls for three generations," she reminded him.

"A fair apprenticeship. But not for those kinds of pearls. Jakways kept a roof over their heads with buttons and doodad earrings and we both know it. You lost your whole family in that fire, didn't you, sweetheart?"

She looked in his eyes and saw nothing but sympathy and neighborly affection, yet the blood skidding through her veins spoke of other messages. *Leave me alone. Please, just leave me alone. What have I ever done to you?* "Mr. Hemming, why did you really ask me here?" she asked him.

"To help you. Nothing more. When you go into the major leagues, Laura, you have to expect to play hardball. How long did you think you were going to be able to keep pearls like those a secret?" He leaned forward, pointing the lighter at her like a finger. "Anyone in hell could walk down to your riverfront. Spill a little oil in your inlets. Flick a match to your lab. You saw the electric fence around my place, the guards. You could be ruined as fast as breathe with the setup you've got."

"Mr. Hemming—" His fingertip rubbed the smooth gold finish, and this time she didn't imagine it. When he pushed the lighter wheel, flame sparked within millimeters of the bud vase centerpiece. Her stomach turned.

Hemming genially smiled at her. "You're wondering why on earth that's any of my business, but of course it is, honey. It's your problem if someone takes a few of your pearls. But it becomes mine if the savvy that went into the necklace of yours got into the wrong hands. It isn't going to do you—or me—one ounce of good to have pearls that quality flood the market a few years down the line. And the fact of the matter is that I'm in a position to help you."

A quick frown pleated her forehead. She shook her head, but before she could say anything he was talking again. "You're so young you could be my daughter, prettier than most women have a right to be. Vulnerable. The image of a match and your lab up in flames made you sick, didn't it? I could see from the look on your face."

Reason, not instinct, mattered. She'd believed that for years. She'd ignored the lighter. She'd ignored the building feeling of uneasiness and the feeling of crabmeat salad settling in her stomach like a cold gray ball, but now she had to face that something was wrong—with this man and this meeting. "I don't know what you're trying to suggest, Mr. Hemming, but—"

"It isn't what I want. It's what you do. You need capital. Protection. And I'm prepared to offer you both of them. I'm even prepared to take you under my wing in return for a nominal kind of partnership—all the advantages on your side. I could teach you more than you've ever dreamed of about pearls, honey, and I've got facilities that could make those blue eyes of yours turn stark green with envy.''

She'd thought she was prepared for anything that could happen at this lunch meeting. Anything but absolutely everything that *was* happening. "You must know that the only asset I could possibly bring to any partnership is my land."

His chuckle was long and low. "The last thing I need is an aging plantation, sweetheart." He motioned to the closed black case to her right. "All I want from you is a little shared information. I want to know what nucleating source you used to produce those kind of pearls. That's not much to ask, is it? In return, look what I have here, what I can offer you in facilities and research...."

"Yes." She set her napkin on the table and reached for her purse. Gently, carefully, she said, "It's a generous offer, but I'm frankly not interested."

Some men turned hot when angry, some cold. Her neighbor's blue eyes suddenly glittered as smooth as skating pond ice. "You're crazy not to be."

"Yes. I know." She tried to explain honestly, because there was no reason not to be honest with him. "I'm afraid I would make a poor business partner for anyone. I've been independent too long. Believe me, I appreciate your offer. It was very kind, and lunch was delicious."

"You're making a mistake." That fast, his tone turned lethally bitter.

She could still taste that bitterness all the way as she walked to her car, and the fingers that grasped the steering wheel were shaking as she left the drive. Only when the wrought iron gates snapped closed behind her could she feel the oxygen pouring into her lungs. Fear was seeping through her veins like an insidious poison.

He'd been kind. Over and over she tried to convince herself that Nat Hemming had been nothing but kind. His offer of a partnership had been wonderfully generous. She craved the chance to learn from a man who knew as much as he did about pearls, and Hemming had the background to be both mentor and teacher. With some solid capital, she could change over her business completely to serious, good quality pearls.

But the man made her skin crawl. She railed at herself the entire way home about idiotic women who made decisions on instinct instead of sound sense. But she couldn't erase the pictures in her mind, pictures Hemming had made a point of creating. An oil slick on her neck of the river could kill all her mussels, destroy her potential pearl business for generations to come. And a fire...visions of fire cramped her mind, visions of searing pain and burns and flames and smoke. He knew about the fire that had taken her parents' life. Dammit, he hadn't been playing with that lighter by accident.

Like her kind, generous, distinguished neighbor said, Mr. Hemming knew how to play hardball.

Her hands were suddenly trembling so hard she had to pull over to the side of the road.

* * *

The wind made one long, low keening moan before a streak of lightning cracked the black sky wide open in the distance.

"Laura. We're getting off the water. Now."

"In a minute. The storm's not that close." Laura never looked up. Knee-deep in river water, she wrestled to separate the mussel cages from the raft. In principle a contemporary pearl grower with up-to-date equipment could accomplish the same job without ever leaving the boat. Her equipment was antiquated, her unwieldy gloves made the project additionally difficult and so did the wire-taut mood that had been chasing her since lunch.

An angry clap of thunder vibrated through the sky, inevitably making her jump, and then she ignored it.

"Laura—"

"I know, I know. It's coming, but I don't want to have to come back to this neck of the river tomorrow night. If we finish here now, we won't have to do that."

Her toes felt grainy in mud; her smoke-gray blouse was sticking to her. Her shoulders ached and her throat was stone dry. But it was like never walking under an open ladder, avoiding black cats. If she worked hard enough, nothing could touch her. It was a simple trade with fate: if the Nat Hemmings in this life would just leave her alone, she'd work harder than two men, never complain of thirst or tiredness, never breathe wrong. She'd do everything right.

"Laura—"

"In a minute!" All afternoon she'd thought about putting a security fence around her property. All afternoon she'd known darn well that fences were no protection against anyone who really wanted to harm her, and that included Hemming. A woman's ability to protect herself was measured in other dynamics— strength of will, smarts, drive, pride. And never letting the opposition know what you were afraid of. Lord, she hated feeling helpless.

Lightning slashed through the night, so silver and bright that she suddenly lifted her head. Then, like a shock of electricity, she felt Nick's hands latch on her waist from behind. The power and strength in his fingers sent awareness sizzling through her that startled her private demons to kingdom come. Her whole body tensed.

Nick waded with his magnolia-skinned booty to the boat, raised her up and plopped her neat bottom with a distinct spank on the seat in the stern. Slowly, he tugged off each of his gloves and tossed them at her, then hauled himself up over the side. A mercilessly hard black gaze drilled through her as he grabbed the oars. The dare between them was so clear she could have touched it.

He hadn't touched her, not in four nights, until that moment. The look in his eyes dared her to make a federal issue out of that.

She dropped her eyes and let an exasperated sigh escape her lips. "I've been a little difficult to work with tonight?" she asked delicately.

"Stubborn, nasty, relentless, slave driving, irrational—"

"Hey. I withdraw the question."

"When's the last time you had a full eight hours' sleep?"

"Are you back to that again? I told you, I never need more than five hours' sleep."

Nick paddled with fast, sure speed, guiding the boat away from open waters. His tone couldn't have been more conversational. "I told you about the years I spent making a fortune on Cambodian jade. Bush shirts and steaming heat, snakes bigger around than a man's arm and jaguars haunting the nights. And the damned jungle—you clear it and overnight it's grown twice as fast by the time you're ready to go the next day. If I ever go back, Laura Jakway, I'm taking you with me. Even with a damn good guide and a crew, the trip is hell—but we won't need the guide or the crew. Just you. You can lead, tote the rifles, battle the jungle and carry the elephants when they get tired. It would undoubtedly be nothing more than a normal day's work for you."

She pushed back her hair and reached for her boots. "It's becoming increasingly difficult to tell when you're being insulting."

"I was being insulting. Now lean back put your feet up and for once don't argue."

"I'll bet you've lost women in your life right and left because of that bossy streak," she remarked.

"*My* bossy streak? How many men in your life couldn't survive a dictator's rule?"

"Hundreds." Her tone was sad, regretful.

And imaginative, Nick thought wryly. He'd spent hours with her now and had seen those turquoise eyes of hers promise the earth and stars when she laughed. He'd seen her in river mud to her neck; he'd heard her soft alto whisper legends and myths about pearls. She'd worked at a pace that no woman could tolerate and had gently coaxed idiotic childhood tales out of him that he'd forgotten and certainly never told anyone before. The scent of her fragile perfume had assailed him and he'd seen the way she touched a rose, then watched her turn around and tote twenty pounds of weed-drenched mussel cages. Laura was all contradictions, beauty and spice, drive and softness, mystery and laughter. The one thing he was absolutely certain of was that she knew little of men.

She'd been startled when he first started bantering with her. Her sense of humor came alive when she was teased, and it was as if no man had had the sense to simply *be* with her. Men and women had played verbal games since the beginning of time, but Laura acted like she just crossed a river and greeted life. A few roses, champagne, lazy talk . . . she was so hungry for it.

Watching her this evening had disturbed him, disarmed him. She'd walked toward him with her chin as stiff as carved white marble and a haunted exhaustion in her eyes. She'd worked like dynamite waiting for the ignition of a fuse, an excuse to explode. He told himself that after so many hours of working together, it was natural he would feel some protective, paternal feelings for her.

That was a crock. He wanted to take a loaded shotgun to whoever the hell had put the desperation in her eyes.

Impatience snapped through him. Maybe the lady with the huge turquoise eyes didn't know it, but she was looking for a man to set down roots with. A man who believed in love and had the capacity for it, one strong and caring enough to see those fragile defenses for what they were.

He'd stopped being that man sometime when he was a kid, shuffled between oceans to land in yet another place where he wasn't wanted. Love was a cheap word people used to bridge the loneliness. He could handle the loneliness.

At least, he always had. Until a week ago. When one small, stubborn, fiercely independent woman had started nagging at him. Teasing him. Talking to him. Laughing with him. And making very sure he understood she wanted nothing from him.

Lightning made another razor slash in the sky, showing the sharp clean backdrop of trees, the mystery shadows of swamp and river. "I love storms," she said absently.

"Most people have a little healthy fear of lightning and water."

Laura rolled down her jeans cuffs and leaned back against the stern. "I've had the brailer out on storms on the river a dozen times. There's nothing like it. The water's like an inky mirror now, but I've seen it when the waters were swelling over the banks and the current was like a rage, leaves crushed in the rain and thunder like a temper...." She shook her head. "Wonderful," she said simply.

"You have a small problem with insanity, Miss Jakway."

"Ah, well." She grinned. "We all have a little something."

He told himself to leave her alone, but the words were already spilling out. "So when are you going to get around to telling me about the 'little something' that upset you today?"

"Nothing happened—"

"Tell me," he repeated softly.

The first fat plop of rain splashed on the seat in front of her. She glanced at the sky and then at Nick, at the way his dark sweatshirt was pushed up at the sleeves and his black jeans molded over long strong thighs. The devil had eyes like Nick's. The devil had that sheen of raven hair, the rigid strong bones, the...sexiness.

All evening she'd had the urge to tell him her problems. She knew he would have listened, and she badly wanted to seek the advice of a man whose opinion she valued, a man she was helplessly beginning to trust.

She hadn't told him anything, and she wouldn't. Her scars were part of that reason and so was pride, but neither totally explained her silence. What held her back was that these long night hours together weren't like real life. They weren't like Hemming and firing Simon and engine repairs and mortgages and nucleating pearls. Roses and a man's dark tenor. The lazy way his eyes rested on her and the gentle teasing. The secret of their pearls and sipping champagne and...dammit, she could handle the Hemmings if she could just have this.

"Laura? Is it a business problem? Or money you're worried about?"

She heard the husky gentleness in his voice and felt angry, helpless. "I can handle my own problems, Nick. This has nothing to do with you or your nutrient formula."

He ignored that. "Because if money's the problem, we can change the terms of the agreement we made. I never needed these pearls—"

"You can forget that. If I was a bag lady living on the streets I wouldn't take your pearls. They're yours, for your grandfather," she said fiercely.

"That's very nice. Now tell me what's wrong."

"Nothing is wrong."

"Then tell me what happened today."

"Lord, you're unbelievable. You just don't let up do you?"

"The lady has every reason to be annoyed. I had no right to pry. Forget I ever said anything."

She drew her knees up, wrapping her arms around them with a massive sigh. The wind was picking up dust and hurling it in the air, turning a black night blacker and isolating the man in front of her in shadows. He'd retreated from her, not in physical but emotional distance. That was safest. Only it hurt. "I don't find it so easy to share," she admitted quietly.

"Neither do I."

"I don't believe on leaning on other people, Nick. I don't want to take anything from you." She hesitated. "These last nights have been . . . nice. For you, too?"

"Yes." He barely murmured the word.

She paused again. "Honesty . . . sometimes it's easier to be honest with a stranger than with people you see every day. That's exactly what's been so nice these last nights, knowing there was a kind of honesty between us that was just . . . free. Uncomplicated.''

She took a deep breath. "And there's no reason for you to be thinking some monumental disaster happened to me today. It wasn't like that. I only ran pell-mell into a personal nemesis of mine. Everyone's got one. Snakes, spiders, storms. A fear that goes beyond rhyme or reason or common sense. I have a terror of fire that I've let my head build into something silly, neurotic.'' She smiled at him suddenly. "And that's all. That's it. It was never worth a mention to begin with. Okay? Can we completely drop the subject now?''

"Laura—Damn!"

After four days of building pressure and clouds, all at once the sky exploded. Nick had a frustrated moment to wonder if she'd arranged the wet deluge. He wouldn't put it past her. Every time he got a little close, every time he edged near Laura Jakway's secrets, she managed to elude him. Fire? What the hell kind of clue was fire?

For now it couldn't matter. For now nothing could matter but getting them both immediately to shelter. A litany of four-letter words filled his head as the sky flung torrents of rainy needles down on them. He instinctively wanted to protect her. It was a need, an emotion that Nick Langg had never had and it terrified him. It had nothing to do with the rain. It had to do with a perfectly crazy princess who'd completely erased the previous moment from her head and was laughing as they pulled to shore.

Leaping to the water at the same time he did, she tossed him the rope, helped him tug the boat up to land, then splashed back for their cache of mussels. She had to shout to be heard over the thunder of rain. "Isn't this terrific?"

What could he say? He saw her dark hair become wet ribbons, softer than ebony, luxuriously lustrous. The water molded her blouse to her skin within seconds, and diamond moisture weighted her lashes. "We've been waiting for this for so long! It's been so hot and dry, and this . . ."

Yes, he could see. In his life, rain was simply a cold wet reality. Laura saw the dusty earth replaced by shine and the leaves dancing for silver lightning. She was so . . . illogical. So different from him. He saw her tongue flick out to taste the rain, and all he could think of was that this was his lady who finally had her defenses down. She took his breath away. "Dammit, would you get over here?" he shouted to her.

"I'm coming, I'm coming."

All at once the earth became skid slick. Their cache of mussels tonight was thankfully light, but still a burden to carry through rain-drenched brush in the pitch black. Lightning splintered the sky. Nick adjusted the rope nets so he could throw an arm around her shoulder, the best he could do to protect her—she stiffened, then relaxed. Earth and life smells, brought out by the rain, assaulted him as they ran. And the rain pounded on the river behind them.

Panting, hot, wet, they reached the porch of her lab out of breath and soaked. Laura slid from under his arm and dropped the mussel nets at her feet; he dropped his. Air was heaving into both their lungs. He saw her lips, moist with rain, the water running down her forehead, clean, soft, pure. She never did wear more makeup than moonlight.

There was no way he could have stopped himself from touching her. He meant nothing, really. He meant to smooth her wet hair from her face, to brush the raindrops on her cheeks. The laughter was still in her eyes; he simply wanted to share a moment more of it.

But she shied, suddenly, pulled back. Her smile died. Maybe because his did. He could see all those careful defenses of hers hauling up drawbridges again, and maybe it was all that elemental sound and fury all around them. He saw the sudden shy fear he hated in her eyes, but suddenly that was all there was.

His palms cradled her face and Laura knew what was coming. His mouth came down, hovered over hers, and then claimed. A deafening clap of thunder and the rush of rain, and all she could hear was the silence, the frantic beating of her heart. *No. Don't. Please, please...*

He tasted of clean, fresh rain. His lips rubbed against hers with the friction of softness. From the moment she'd met him, she knew Nick didn't understand...about patience. He took, expecting her to take back. He took her mouth, teasing her with textures and tastes and pressure.

He stepped closer. Both of them were rain slick, her breasts were cold and wet, painfully firm when they crushed against his chest. His hands slid into her hair, lifting the damp weight, then stole down, to her nape, her shoulders, her spine.

She was so tired. So tired of being afraid. Tired of being alone, of being proud. The rain confused everything. It seemed natural to want him. It seemed natural to want to be touched. His kisses were like wet silk and she found herself clinging, blindly, helplessly.

He was so lean, so strong. He kissed with lips, tongue, teeth. He kissed like this was his first kiss, his last kiss. He took her mouth and he molded it beneath his, and she found her fingers climbing in his rain-wet hair.

It was his fault she couldn't regain sanity. Need shuddered through his body and she saw his eyes, black, glazed, lonely. She'd been alone too long, but she suddenly understood—so had he.

Yield was a reckless, abandoned sensation that encompassed night and lightning and the endless hushed pounding of rain. She felt his tongue, sweeping the sweetness from the secret corners of her mouth. She felt his hands, restless, sliding down to her hips and molding her tight and hard against him. She felt desire like a rage. She felt wonder. She felt explosions of no in her head and didn't care.

The taste of *just once* was so sweet, so fierce. To give in to pure lush sensation . . . she never had, never could, but Nick was the lure of the forbidden. She wanted his hands on the intimate flesh of her bottom. She wanted to feel the hard force of his arousal. Her neck ached from the pressure of his mouth and she wanted to feel that ache. He could have . . . anything.

Mouth, wrists, toes, cells. She didn't care. She hurt everywhere. He was the cause.

When he tore his mouth from hers, she felt terrifyingly weak. Startled. She felt the pads of his thumbs suddenly, slowly tracing the line of her cheekbones. His breath heaved between them. "I want you," he hoarsely whispered. "I've no right to ask, but I'm asking you, Laura. Let me love you."

Chapter 5

The rain was still slushing down. All she saw were Nick's eyes, passion-black, waiting. His words, Let me love you, echoed in her mind. A thousand emotions suddenly welled inside her—wanting, hope, despair, wonder, need, something shared and intimate that had no name and didn't need one.

She touched his cheek and stepped back. "I can't," she said softly.

"Why?"

"I can't," she repeated. It wasn't an answer, not after what they'd just shared, but it was all she had. She had to look away from those eyes.

She fumbled in her pocket for her lab key. As if nothing had happened between them, she opened the door, made sure the blinds were closed, flicked on a light and started to drag in the mussels. The nets made instant puddles on the floor; she stepped over them and reached for a black sweatshirt on a hook. She tossed it to Nick without looking at him. "Over the years, those hooks keep reproducing clothes like rabbits," she said with a blithe cheerfulness. "Heaven knows who that belongs to, but at least it's something warm and dry for you to put on. You have to be as soaked as I am. Anyway, if you want it, it's there. I'll be right back."

She disappeared into the small bathroom off the lab and locked the door. Outside the rain had felt warm and welcomed; now her skin felt damp and chill. Blind, fast, she unbuttoned and peeled off her gray blouse. Her bra was just as soaked; she stripped that off, too. Over the years she'd worked too long in all weather conditions not to stock a shelf with spare clothes. Her fingers snatched a white turtleneck and dark sweatshirt, and then she turned.

A small mirror hung over the sink. She caught her frozen smile in the reflection, a smile that died fast and painfully. Cold and wet, the scars on her throat and right breast showed up angry, bright, stark. Red was the color of pain.

She closed her eyes, pulled on the turtleneck, carefully adjusted the collar, then tugged on the sweatshirt. Fury vibrated through her for her foolishness. She knew exactly what she'd invited with Nick in the darkness. She knew exactly what she'd invited in all those light, casual conversations with Nick for all the past nights.

She'd wanted to feel his mouth on hers. She'd wanted to feel wrapped up in his arms. Nick would be a reckless, passionate lover. Demanding. Impatient. She wanted that, too.

Every dream she'd had for nights had been colored by him. She'd dreamed that he needed her, that he wouldn't care that she wasn't experienced. She'd dreamed that she was special to him, that he'd found an honesty and easiness with her he'd never found with another woman, that she could teach him trust because she knew so much about loneliness and pride herself.

They were dreams of a fool. She attacked her wet hair mercilessly with a brush, turning away from the mirror. *Why don't you just strip, Laura? Walk out there and show him how pretty those scars are. We could put an end to those idiotic fantasies so fast it would make your head spin.*

She thought of Nick's eyes clouded with pity and felt sick.

By the time she walked back out in the lab, Nick had filled a beaker with water for coffee and started working. They'd worked out a tandem set of tasks in the nights past. He pried open the mussels, dealt with the mess; she extracted the pearls, carefully cleaned and then analyzed them.

From the beginning, Nick knew she hadn't liked the arrangement. If it was up to Laura, she'd be doing it all, and when she stepped out of the bathroom he saw that she'd slipped on a perfectionist mood.

Sweatshirts were meant to be comfortably baggy; hers fit neat and trim. The ridge of her shoulders would have lined up to a ruler, and the carefully cheerful smile was exhaustingly regal. "We have a lot to do.'' She had the busiest eyes, pouncing on everything but him. ''We may have a short haul because of stopping early, but it looks like a good catch, don't you think?''

He briefly considered hauling her down to the cold muddy floor. The throb of desire was still reeling through him. The lady who'd released fire in the rain had gone back into hiding. He wanted her back. He wanted the shape of her beneath him and the feel of her skin beneath his hands. He wanted to know why fire made her afraid. Once he learned all the things that had ever made her afraid he would protect her from them.

Guilt snapped into his conscience. Maybe the only thing Laura Jakway needed protecting from was him—a man who was leaving her life in two weeks, a man who knew nothing of caring, who'd never even believed in love.

So he said nothing, and they worked in silence for nearly an hour. By the time Nick was cleaning up, Laura had switched on the special lighting over the work counter. She slipped the black spectroscope band over her head and adjusted the magnifying loupe to study their night's crop of pearls.

The loupe magnified each pearl ten times. In each one, she searched for blisters, pimples, cavities and horizontal lines—all particularly common flaws in cultureds.

She didn't jump when she felt Nick's hand on her shoulder. Instead, every cell in her body went carefully still. ''Well? What's the judgment on tonight's loot?'' he asked casually.

"They're perfect." Normally, this was the best part of her day, the moments that had been sustaining her though rough hours, personal work problems and even all her confusion about Nick. His pearls were so important. Tonight, though, she pushed up the loupe and sighed with exasperation. "Nick, you don't understand how impossible this is."

"So tell me."

"Cultured pearls almost always tend to be spherical in shape, not round. And cultureds are never this deep charcoal-black unless they're dyed. I don't care what kind of pearls you're talking about, no oyster produces pearls of the same uniform color. And size is another thing. In part, size of a pearl is obviously affected by the size of the shell nucleus it started with, but even so—some of your pearls have been up to ten millimeters. It's completely impossible to produce a ten millimeter pearl in three years' time."

"Except in color, they don't look very different to me than the pearls that came out of your control mussels last night." The look she shot him contained a schoolmarm's thoroughly appalled reaction to a pupil's blind ignorance. Nick almost smiled. Instead, a frown gradually pinched between his brows. "You believe the formula had an effect, don't you?" he asked slowly.

"The first night I didn't, no. And all these nights, I haven't really been sure, Nick. I was very careful where I planted these mussels. I chose the youngest, healthiest species. The temperature and PH of the water—everything could have affected good pearls, and those same exact set of conditions I'd never worked with before. Even that first night, I knew your formula had affected color, but the quality—"

"You thought the quality was a fluke?"

"I thought it was everything we did, plus a good dose of chance and luck." She turned away from him, carefully slotting each pearl in its own protective sack.

"Still, you can't be sure it's the formula."

"I'm sure. Mr. Langg, you have a potential fortune on your hands so big that I can't even fathom the scope of it." She made the comment with a smile, hoping to earn one back. Her mind, for once, simply wasn't on pearls, but she'd hope that their work and their talk would divert Nick from pursuing what had happened outside.

For the moment, however, she couldn't see his expression. He'd taken the sack of pearls and was peeling up the invisible hinged section of the floor beneath her desk. Her small underground vault was made of steel and concrete two layers thick. She'd already assured him that it would survive even if fire or earthquake leveled her lab. She crossed the room and bent down at the same time he moved away.

"It's past time I told you the combination," she told him.

"It'll wait." He switched off her counter light and reached for his damp sweatshirt.

"You should know, Nick. If something happens to me—"

"Nothing's going to happen to you, Laura." If he knew nothing else, he was positive of that. As the size of their pearl cache grew, the back of his mind had started cataloging problems and possibilities that would inexorably have to be dealt with, and soon. He'd never planned on incredible complications rising from this simple experiment of his grandfather's.

He hadn't planned on his growing feelings for the lady standing stubbornly by the door, chin up and pride snapping, so wary he was going to touch her that she was frozen.

It would have helped him a great deal if he could have banished images of dragons chasing princesses from his mind. He still didn't know what she was afraid of.

He would learn.

He flicked open her blinds and took one last look at her lab with a fussy glance that he'd learned from his hundred-and-ten pound nemesis. Everything was in place, pristine and white and clean again. He stepped closer to her then and flicked out the last light.

The storm had eased to a silky silent downpour by the time they stepped out on the porch. Laura locked the door and turned. Nick was suddenly inches from her. His palms captured her face, forced her eyes up to his. She froze, startled by the blaze of frustration on his face, the leashed power in those hands that had no intention of letting her move.

"Stop it, Laura."

"I don't know what you—"

"Of course you do. I asked you no more than the same simple question that man has been asking woman since the beginning of time. A woman has a right to say no with no explanations, no embarrassment, no apologies. Dammit, do you really think I was the kind of man who would force you? *Don't* be afraid of me."

She breathed, slowly and carefully, when he dropped his hands. "All right." They were the only words that seemed capable of escaping her lips.

"Say it."

"I'm not afraid of you," she said quietly, and suddenly meant it. The kaleidoscope of emotions Nick aroused in her was complex, upsetting, powerful. But fear that he would ever have forced a sexual relationship that she didn't want had never existed. It couldn't.

The taut lines in his face suddenly eased. A glimmer of a smile played at the corners of his mouth. "I may have hurt people over the years," he said softly. "But never deliberately. And never you. Laura?"

"We have to go. It's nearly dawn."

His palm claimed her wrist and the pad of his thumb lingered on her pulse, heating the blood in her veins. All she could think of was that she'd never be able to stand on her lab porch, never see rain again, without remembering the thick, sweet clot of emotions this man's touch aroused in her.

"You didn't say no, Laura. 'I can't' is something else entirely. And until I find out why you can't, that door's still open."

She shook her head. "You're only going to be here for another week, at the most two—"

"I'll be here for as long as it takes."

"For the pearls, you mean."

He didn't answer her.

* * *

"You're going to be gone two days, Sam?"

"Or one long one. It's a five hour drive there and back, plus the time to crate up the blacks."

"Blacks! Washboards, Pigtoes! Can't the two of you talk anything but oysters?" Mattie wagged a finger at both of them. "I'm ashamed of both of you, all this talk about breeding habits in the middle of a supper table. Manners has gotten way out of hand around here."

"You're absolutely right." Laura exchanged glances with Sam, then wordlessly helped cart dinner plates to the table. The roast was simmering with carrots and onions; steam wisped from the bowl of mashed potatoes. Butter-browned rolls were served with honey and a spinach salad shined with Mattie's favorite dressing.

For a few minutes, there was nothing more than, "This is wonderful, Mattie" and "This is the best meal I've had in weeks, Mattie" and "Pass the butter, please, Mattie."

Mattie's sigh was as weary as a March wind. "All right. Get on with it before you both drive me crazy."

Sam immediately leaned both elbows on the table and downed an entire roll in a gulp. "The core of the harvest should be done in another three days."

"Yes, but I don't want the crew gone yet, Sam. Every one of the flat-bottoms needs a paint and an overhaul, and there's at least a couple weeks of equipment repair beyond that."

"I've got all winter to handle some of that, but you're getting a new engine in the brailer this fall because I'm going to drown the old one myself."

"She's still running," Laura protested.

"Running? That motor hasn't *run* in three and a half years. It only keeps going through a sheer contrary nature. Takes after its boss."

"Thanks for nothing. Mattie, do not sneak another roll on this plate. When I'm two hundred pounds and waddling you're going to be completely responsible—and I'll sit down with the books this week, Sam. Take a look at cash flow...."

Mattie spooned potatoes on Laura's plate and heaped two more slices of meat on Sam's. Neither of them heard the sharp rap on the front door; she didn't expect them to. When those two got talking seriously, cows could graze in the kitchen and neither would notice. Although she hoped they'd notice her cherry pie or she'd kill them both without a twinge of conscience. Wiping her hands on her apron, she stalked out of the kitchen toward the front door.

Nick hadn't necessarily expected Laura to answer his knock, but he'd never had the impression that Laura's Mattie was quite such a glowering old biddy. "Is Miss Jakway in?"

"Miss Jakway is eating dinner. What can I do for you?"

"I would appreciate your telling her I was here." He didn't have a rank and serial number to offer her. His tone was apologetic, but only with an effort. As princess-guarders went, the scowling old nag was so good he was tempted to grin. He added dryly, "I'm not selling anything. She knows me. May I come in?"

"What's the name?"

"Nick. Langg." His name seemed to produce a minor miracle. She not only released her hold on the door, but gave him a fast, thorough head-to-toe inspection. When she smiled, her age dropped from a crotchety 310 to a respectably young sixty.

"I've heard the name. Laura's already told me to make sure she got any calls that came in from you. You can come in." She shot him another look. "And since you're here, you might as well have some dinner."

"That's not necessary—"

"Certainly it's necessary. If you don't eat, then she'll stop eating and she forgets half her meals as it is. Besides that, dinner's the most interrupted meal we have around here. I learned a long time ago to make enough for extras. Now come on in, come on in. We don't stand on formality in this house. What did you say your business was?"

She got in eight fast questions before they crossed the doorway to the kitchen. Nick, amused, considered that she could have applied for a job as a game show host. He didn't quite figure out her sudden enthusiasm until she stepped in the kitchen ahead of him with a flourishing gesture, as if presenting Laura with a fatted calf. "Mr. Langg. The poor thing hasn't had dinner and here it is past seven o'clock. We'll just fix you a plate right next to Laura here."

"Nick!"

He saw surprise shock color into Laura's cheeks, but was more immediately diverted by the grizzly giant sitting across from her. While Mattie slid dishes in front of him, Laura seemed to catch her breath, and then made fast introductions. Sam slid half out of his chair to extend a hand. The man's raw brawn handshake packed power. Another princess protector?

But not one who liked strangers showing up at Laura's dinner table. Nick had heard Laura mention her foreman's name often enough to know she totally, implicitly, trusted Sam. His first judgment was the opposite. Sam was hulking big, with intimidating taciturn features and shoulders barely contained by a frayed work shirt. The bulk and brawn were fine, but the man's eyes were clammed up tight with hostility.

"Well, now," Mattie beamed. "We don't have to talk oysters for a few minutes."

One of three was remarkably easy to please. "I haven't had a roast this delicious in years," Nick said honestly.

"For you, a giant piece of cherry pie. You like cherry pie?"

"I love cherry pie."

Nick doubted Mattie made a regular habit of stuffing men who arrived on Laura's doorstep. Everything about her behavior, and Sam's, led him to believe that strangers rarely darkened the old plantation's doors. Mattie obviously wished they did; Sam wished the grounds were surrounded by barbed wire. Both were sneaking regular glances at Laura.

Old dishes whisked out of sight and new ones whisked in. Dinner turned into pie; iced tea turned into coffee. When the last plates were scraped and the last cup emptied, Sam was still sprawled in his seat at the table and Mattie was still clinging to her empty cup.

Bemused, Laura cupped her chin in her hands and waited. Both Sam and Mattie would normally have flown in opposite directions a good fifteen minutes earlier at any normal meal. Instead, curiosity was picking up in the room like dust for a vacuum and three people in the room were trying very hard to figure out why Nick was here.

Laura headed that pack. The last she knew, Nick had been fairly violent on the subject of secrecy for his project. She had no idea why he'd changed the rules.

But then, two nights ago he'd changed a lot of rules. Two nights ago his hair had been rain-slicked ebon, instead of thick and smooth brushed coal like now. Two nights ago he'd been wearing a ragged, borrowed sweatshirt, not a cream-striped tailored shirt like tonight. And two nights ago those cool quiet eyes had possessed the naked glow of passion. The man had been coming apart from emotion. He showed no emotion now. Courtesy was no effort for him, but he was no prey for vultures.

He was the falcon instead, vibrantly aware, listening, still. He never failed to answer a question. He never gave a thing away.

As a man, he fascinated her. She was determined to believe that wasn't the same thing as fear, and enough was enough.

"Well now..." Mattie finally stirred. "Best get these dishes done."

"I've been meaning to fix the screen on the back door." Sam stood up.

"Good night, Mattie, Sam," Laura said cheerfully. "Mattie, I'll do the dishes. And Sam, you've never fixed a screen door in your life. We'll say goodnight, and I'll see you both in the morning."

She had to suffer a few more minutes. Sam made a point of mentioning to Nick that he'd be close by if either of them needed anything. Mattie did her best to fuss with dishes until Laura took a plate from her hands and replaced it with Mattie's worn purse.

Rather suddenly, they were gone and silence flooded the kitchen. A peach sunset glowed from the west windows as Laura filled the sink with soapy water. "Would you like an after-dinner brandy?"

"If you have some."

"In the pantry, the bottom shelf. Glasses to my left here, up above." She cleared the table and whisked a wrap over the leftovers. It seemed odd, doing such mundane things around him. They'd never done ordinary things together. Pearling in mist and moonlight, champagne and roses, and going stark raving mad in the rain two nights ago. But sometime, somewhere, someone always had to do dishes. If she didn't look at him, maybe she could convince herself that her feelings for Nick were just as ordinary.

He set a glass filled with amber liquid near the sink by her. "Mattie's been trying to marry you off for a long time?"

She chuckled. "Five years, give or take."

"With that kind of pressure, I'm surprised you haven't succumbed." He liked that she made no apology for her friend.

"Contrary to all Southern traditions, I've decided I won't shrivel up and die if I stay single." To her total shock, he picked up a towel and stole the dripping blue delft plate from her hands.

"You're against marriage?"

"For me."

"Burned once?"

It was an unfortunate choice of words, though Nick couldn't know that. "Mattie would tell you that I've worked myself into the unmarriageable category," she said lightly. "Too independent, too stubborn. My cooking skills are pushed with peanut butter sandwiches. And I can probably keep up a silly conversation as long as you can, but I doubt you came here for that."

While she drained the sink, he dried her roasting pan, thinking that he'd started the "silly conversation" to postpone upsetting her as long as he could. Instead, he'd succeeded in upsetting himself. From the very beginning, it would have been easier if she was married. Or engaged. Or even if he had one sound reason to believe she was involved with a man.

She was wearing a watercolor-pastel blouse tonight, ice-blue slacks, and, not expecting him, she'd worn her hair loose and free to her shoulders. Coal dust was the color, silk the texture.

She was fast running out of patience. "Nick, you've avoided contact with the people I work with since you've been here. I'm delighted you changed the rules—I've been telling you from the first that you could trust Sam and Mattie. But you were the one so concerned with secrecy—''

''I still am. But the circumstances have changed, Laura.''

''How?'' Her tone reeked frustration.

''Pick up your brandy. Let's settle somewhere.''

She chose the living room. An antique mirror hung over the marble mantle, and the colors were French blue and peach. Nothing in the room was new, but like everything he associated with Laura, the room reflected a uniquely feminine love for perfection and beauty. Warmth. Maybe because his life had so lacked it, he was predominantly aware that she brought that quality to everything around her.

And she was holding that brandy glass like it would protect her from dragons.

''Drink the brandy,'' he said quietly.

''For heaven's sake—''

''Laura, I want to call off the experiment.''

Something slammed into her chest, cold and sharp. ''You can't mean that! Nick, we haven't finished half the harvest. If it's because you have to leave, you can leave. I can do all the work; you don't have to be involved. You never really had to be involved to begin with; I just—''

''That's not why.'' Nick's brooding eyes met hers from halfway across the room. ''Listen to me.''

''I *am* listening.''

''And take a sip of that brandy!''

"I don't want the brandy!" She jammed the glass on a low mahogany side table, and wrapped her arms around her waist.

He sighed, keeping his voice low, soothing, patient. "You know why I entered this project—for my grandfather. In a sense that debt was paid from the time Heroshi's impossible nutrient was tested. My grandfather was never interested in wealth, but dreams."

"But that's just it. This isn't a dream; it's real, Nick. It *works*. You've seen the pearls—"

"What I see is that I've put you in a position of risk. Never what I intended or ever expected could happen."

"I don't understand."

She sank down to the window seat, framed in the last of a peach and mauve sunset. The room was darkening minute by minute. Nick found the switch on one lamp, then another. Creating the small pools of light gave him something to do besides face the blaze in her angry blue eyes. She wasn't going to listen.

Still, he tried to make her understand. "I've spent most of yesterday and today on long-distance phone calls, checking into what I should have thoroughly investigated three years ago and simply didn't. Truthfully, it never once occurred to me that my grandfather's formula was more than a pipe dream, and maybe this one experiment isn't conclusive, but the results—neither of us expected the results we've had so far. Those results have to be faced. Real and potential control of pearl quality, Laura. It's no game. Suddenly we're talking about something that has the serious ability to affect the entire international pearl market.''

"In a good way. A wonderful way—"

"In a dangerous way," he said quietly. "There were a great many things I didn't understand until I asked the right people the right questions, until I understood what we might be dealing with. The nature of the formula makes it impossible to safeguard. A patent on the process would only be nominal protection, because anyone who had access to the formula could analyze and use it, and the resulting pearls would tell no tales. Short and sweet, we're talking risks for you as long as you're involved that I'm simply not prepared to take.''

"You can't—"

"I want to destroy the formula."

She sprang from the seat, her mind whirling, blood rushing to her head. *"No,"* she said fiercely.

"I don't see another choice."

"No! You're not thinking, Nick. You can't turn down a potential fortune just like that. At least think of the money—"

The smallest slash of a smile curved into his cheeks. "That's almost an amusing argument, coming from you. When you touch a pearl, Laura, the last thing in your head is a dollar sign. You were never motivated to be involved in this because of a potential fortune, and neither was I. But I can at least understand the push and pull of money. I've chased that god half my life. Money, power, control..." A dark look of loneliness shuttered his eyes. "I'll probably still chase that god when this is over. But not for this. There are few risks I wouldn't be willing to take for myself, but not for you. There's a point where no promise of wealth can justify the risks involved."

Emotions shivered through her—frustration, fury, fear. She'd seen Nick wet, dry, cold, aching tired, snapping alert, sleepy. She'd seen him intimidatingly distant and she'd seen him fiery with desire. She'd spent hours upon hours with this man under conditions that had forced a relationship whether she wanted it or not. It all should have meant something. There had to be a key to get through to him. "Your pearls are perfect, Nick. How can you not understand that they're worth any risk? And dammit, I don't care about me—"

"I do."

The two words were bold, bare. She felt her breath catch at the sudden look in his eyes. She'd pushed a button she shouldn't have pushed. Nick was all through arguing.

He was also moving toward her. Every reason he'd leveled at her for stopping their experiment was rationally sound. It had taken him more time than it should have to gain a total understanding of what he had involved Laura in. Only the naive could believe they could keep their pearl formula a secret. Unless Laura was completely uninvolved, he had no way to protect her.

And unless he got out of her life, he had no way to protect her in another, completely different arena. The lady captivated him. He'd never wanted that to happen. He'd spent afternoons reminding himself of other women who'd kept him happy in bed. He had nothing to offer Laura, nothing she wanted, and he'd thought about his life—a life split between two cultures, a loneliness implicit in his chosen life-style that had no answers, no bridge. From the moment he'd met her, he'd tried to put a name on the reason why she'd so obsessed him. He had no names. To hell with names.

He wanted her. And he was going to pursue her unless he simply left, now, fast, completely.

He stood close enough to breathe her perfume, and touched the hair she would never have left down if she'd known he was coming. His fingers slid through the ebony strands, clenched the softness helplessly, pulling her closer. *Have the sense to move away, Laura. Now. Because if you don't . . .*

But she didn't. She couldn't. Awareness shimmered through her; instincts of danger danced to life. He was warm, close, male. And the promise was unspoken—if she gave up the pearls, every emotional risk this man represented to her would be gone.

But suddenly nothing was simple. She saw stark, harsh pain in his face. Anger. Something desperate and completely unexpected. Need, raw and bitter and sharp.

She tasted that need when his mouth possessed hers. Her whole body went still; her senses went reeling. The gentleness she knew in Nick was gone. He wanted her to feel fear. He moved in like a wall, an unpenetrable chest crushing her breasts, the bold length of his thighs stark against her soft, smaller shape. He anchored her face with hands that gave no quarter, and his mouth . . . ravished. There was no other word. Desire wasn't always pretty, his kiss told her. Desire could be primitive. Raw. Angry. Unwanted. *This is Nick Langg, too, Laura. And I'm not always a pretty man.*

It wasn't a choice that her hands slid carefully up his arms to his shoulders, but a need to gentle him. She felt as if her scars pulsed beneath her silk blouse. She had never been more aware of them. She felt his tongue draining her mouth of moisture, felt his intruding hardness intimately press against her. Still, her lips yielded beneath his. Her fingers glided into his scalp, softly, expressing wonder at the thick heavy texture of his hair.

In those explosive short moments, she understood he was a far more complex man than she'd fathomed, driven by demons she had no knowledge of, chased by ghosts maybe even more powerful than her own. None of that mattered. He needed someone at that moment. He needed a woman who wouldn't walk away from him. He might think he could motivate her with fear. She knew she could motivate him with softness.

His breath suddenly rasped between them. His fingers slid down, rubbing, molding her flesh. Her heart beat, beat, beat when the palms encountered the sides of her breasts. Wake up, Laura, a voice inside her cried.

But she didn't want to. His touch had changed, she could feel it. The heat in her veins was the most basic celebration in being female. She felt rich. She felt whole. The woman in her came alive, and the woman in her trembled helplessly when his hand claimed her breast. Lord, it hurt, and exactly at that moment Nick's touch turned impossibly gentle. Her breast was taut and aching, swollen to the point of pain. The slide

of his fingers over silk was no barrier. All the silk
did—

Was cover scars.

Tears suddenly burned behind her closed eyes.
Nick's hands lifted. His forehead nudged her forehead and his fingertips touched her cheeks. They both
breathed harsh and low. "Laura, I'm sorry," he
whispered. "I never—*never*—meant to hurt you."

"You didn't."

"You're beautiful. I touch you and I can't think.
Your skin is too soft. The scent you wear and your
mouth...your smiles, Laura. Your eyes. I don't know
what you do to me. Dammit, I'm not a gentle man.
I've never been a gentle man—"

He lifted his head, as if those fierce black eyes of
hers demanded that she confirm it. She couldn't. Nick
had the capacity for more gentleness than any man she
had ever known.

"Your lips are red." His thumb traced the bottom
one. "I hurt you."

"No." She breathed once. "No," she repeated, and
then whispered firmly, hopelessly, "But I can't sleep
with you. No affair, Nick. This keeps happening, and
it can't."

He let her step back and away from him. She was
shaky, and her hair tumbled sleepily around her face.
She looked vulnerable and the power this woman had
over him shook Nick. It wasn't the first time she'd
used the word can't. This princess used that word like
it was a moat and a drawbridge. Every time he bridged
her defenses, she retreated to the castle.

"Laura?"

She didn't want to meet his eyes.

"Do you want me to stay or go?"

The honesty of such a simple question shouldn't carry such impossible tangles. Since she couldn't answer the question he asked, she answered the one he didn't. "I don't want you to drop the experiment. I want you to stay for the pearls. I think it's too soon to judge anything until the harvest is over and until we've had all your pearls appraised."

His dark eyes rested on her face, brooding, intense. No, said his common sense. She was technically correct in that it was too soon to make a totally accurate judgment call on the nutrient experiment. All the facts weren't in, but there were enough for a man to know that honor was involved. The honorable choice was to take no chances that Laura could be exposed to danger and risk.

Honor sifted through his head like dust in the wind. He knew damn well he wasn't leaving her. He'd known it before he walked in.

"I guessed you wouldn't be willing to give up the experiment, Laura, and that's why I met your Mattie and Sam. Timing isn't going to change the decisions that have to be made—not when we're only talking a difference of days. We'll finish the harvest if it means that much to you."

She breathed easier for the first time in what seemed like a million hours.

Nick shook his head. "Only I want it done now, Laura. Fast. Not just the harvest but the appraisal of the pearls. And if you're going to be totally involved at that level, obviously you have to be in a position to shift business responsibilities onto your staff." The last word came out on a wry note. A nosy granny and a broody bouncer type—more and more he was beginning to understand exactly how much Laura handled alone. *Langg, this has all the makings of a very bad decision....*

Laura was already looking far too elated. "I can easily shift my work load, and there's nothing to worry about with Sam and Mattie. I'll just tell them I've been doing some private work for you. They don't have to know about your formula. And Nick, I know I can make you change your mind. Once we're done and you've seen all the potential—"

"Potential?" His smile was dry. He touched her cheek, once, lingering. "Potential is exactly and the only reason I'm willing to stay. And I'm not talking about pearls."

"Nick—"

He whispered the order: "Tell me to go. Tell me no. Honey, you have all those choices. All you have to do is make them."

Fuzz collected in her throat, blocking the passage of air and words. She desperately wanted him to go. She couldn't let him stay. Only she also desperately wanted his pearls. Now more than ever in her life that dream of perfect pearls had meaning. There would be no Nick for her, no man. Nick would leave in time and all she'd have, all she could have, were pearls. Something perfect, something beautiful and unflawed to hold on to. She needed his pearls, not Nick. She needed his pearls because of Nick.

Her silence, in time, eased the waiting stillness in Nick's eyes. He smiled suddenly. "I'll see you tomorrow." And then he was striding from the room, and gone.

Chapter 6

Nick's boots crunched on gravel as he crossed the deserted yard to Laura's lab. The hour was daybreak and his mood was brittle. Five sleepless nights in a row had taught him what he already knew. He had absolutely no tolerance for frustration.

Technically, his work was no source of frustration: one more day and this harvest project would be wrapped up. Laura had already set up appointments with two dealers to appraise their pearls in New York for the day after that. The fast timing both suited him and drove him crazy.

He wanted the pearl project done; he wanted to get back to his own world, his own life, his own business.

Only he couldn't leave her. Five days of working beside Laura had confirmed what before had been only vague suspicions and intuition. She was in some kind of serious trouble.

A man with means could easily pick up factual information if he wanted it. He'd done that. He knew now about the fire that had taken her parents' life, and he knew the kind of debt load she'd inherited. He'd learned that she was active in social and community activities in the winter, and that a man named Hank Shull had unsuccessfully been trying to corner her attention for more than a year. If one was to believe the townspeople in Silverwater, Laura was a quiet, gentle lady with her share of pluck and not an enemy in sight.

Maybe she had no enemies, but fear was the hardest emotion to hide. He'd spent the last five days at her side. A fire that had taken place eight years ago didn't begin to explain the here and now anxiety that chased her days. Someone who upset her kept telephoning. Yesterday that foreman of hers had done something or said something that had turned her face stark white.

It was tough to infiltrate Rapunzel's tower when the lady refused to let down her hair.

And a man didn't worry this much about a woman who didn't matter to him, but his conscience was tired of that litany. She didn't want him involved, although he was tired of telling himself that, too.

What in *hell* was he going to do about her?

Her work yard was deserted and would be until eight. He wanted time, coffee and a place to think in silence. As soon as he turned the key to the lab, though, he realized that two out of three were impossible.

The same lady who'd blithely promised to sleep in this morning had already made fresh strong coffee,

and heaven knew how long she'd been up and working. Her lab looked like a cyclone had hit it.

His razor edge of a mood started shifting the instant her chair spun around and her face tilted to his.
It was that damned smile. She was always doing dangerous things like that. Smiling. Welcoming him with
warmth she took for granted and a you-won't-hurt-me
assurance that tested a man's sanity.

"You lied," he announced as he clipped the door
closed behind him.

"A little white fib isn't the same thing as a lie." Her
blouse was the same color as her eyes, and her eyes
had a guilty expression.

"It is in my book. You promised not to set foot in
this lab until eight o'clock this morning."

"For work. This isn't exactly work, Nick. I just had
one little project I wanted to tackle before we finished
our harvest today."

"Little project?" He motioned expressively to the
disaster around her. "Exactly how many hours have
you been up?"

"You need coffee," she said swiftly. "This isn't
going to take me much longer. Grab a mug and I'll
show you what nucleating mussels is all about."

Nick reached for a mug, thinking that he'd seen,
smelled and touched more oysters than any man
needed to in a lifetime. An array of odd-looking tools
littered her counter, and two carts were rolled in front
of her. It seemed like a zillion live mussels were
crowded on racks, and he hadn't had the first sip of
coffee before Laura waved some kind of lethal-looking
probe at him.

"This is absolutely the most exciting part of my work, Nick. Just watch."

"I'm watching." But all he could think of was that the princess only forgot her drawbridge defenses when she was working with her babies.

"See? When the mussels are crowded together, they naturally relax and open up. When they do that, you use a wedge—like this—to keep them from closing, then a clamp to pry them just a little wider. All you need is the space to insert a shell nucleus...."

He cared in the sense that he understood how much her work meant to her. He was simply more interested in other things.

She rarely wore her jeans snugly. This pair must be old, because the blue-white denim caressed her long thighs and hips as intimately as a man's hands would want to. Her skin had that morning freshness, a glow. She'd washed her hair with something that smelled like strawberries. Her blouse had a simple ruffle at the throat, and Nick found an increasing fascination with those high-necked blouses of hers. He'd never noticed women's clothes, except as an awareness that a woman made an individual statement about herself in her choice of styles. In always covering herself, Laura said something about demure, modest, old-fashioned values. That was fine. Except that Nick was gradually building up an obsession about baring her white throat. Soon.

Laura flashed him a quick frown. "Were you listening? If you're not interested—"

"Of course I'm interested." He promptly did his best to look fascinated.

"I don't want to bore you."

"Laura, I heard every word you said. There are two ways to nucleate a mussel. One is by inserting a shell bead. The second way is to snip a bit of live mussel and implant it in another." He mentally blessed his powers of concentration.

And then he blessed hers, because when he leaned over her shoulder she didn't instantly pull away from him. He'd never met a more careful woman than Laura...except when elation and animation for her work made her forget her inhibitions.

"So those are the two concepts, but what's exciting, Nick—where the real potential for producing beautiful pearls comes from—is when you marry the two techniques. See? What you do is nucleate a live mussel with a real pearl from another species...."

"What species?"

She looked delighted he'd asked. "That's part of the wonder—crossbreeding to determine exactly how mussel species affects quality. But in this case, I'm working with *hyriopsis schiegeli*."

"Ah." He resisted the urge to trace the shell of her ear with his fingertip.

"They're an old reliable standard."

"I see."

"Do you want to try one?"

"God, no."

She glanced up at him, and suddenly chuckled—a low throaty feminine chuckle designed to stir a man's hormones. "It's all right to admit it, you know."

She couldn't be that perceptive. "Admit what?"

"That listening to all my constant talking about pearls bores you to bits. You don't have to be so nice, Nick. Just tell me to keep quiet. I'm not trying to put you through torture."

She did that by breathing, something both his heart rate and hormones had already discussed that morning. Suddenly, his eyes met with hers for a clash of a second. A dangerous unnameable emotion sizzled between them. That fast, she shifted away from him with another one of those smiles that made him want to shake her. How could one woman look both warm and wary at the same time?

"Sam promised to finish up here when he got in. I just have a little more I have to do before the two of us head out. You've got time for one more half cup of coffee if you want it—" She stopped talking when she noticed Sam's hulking form in the doorway. One look at her foreman's face and she felt nerves clutter in her stomach. "You're early today, too, Sam."

"Been in the yard a half hour." Sam took a glance at Nick and then motioned to her. "I need to see you a minute outside."

"Fine." Her voice cheerful, she motioned to the coffee again for Nick. "I won't be long."

She grabbed a rag to wipe her hands and followed Sam to the lab porch. If he hadn't closed the door behind her, she would have, ensuring the privacy of their conversation from Nick.

"We got a problem," Sam told her.

She'd already guessed that from the look on his face. "What now?"

"Engine blown on the pickup. Seems someone decided to add a little sugar water to the gas tank."

She finished wiping her hands. An oriole was prancing from limb to limb on the catalpa in the yard. The sun was high and bright and a brilliant yellow. The whole day promised to be glorious. "Damn," she whispered.

"Abe said he saw Simon Howard walking down the side road of the property two days ago."

"He wasn't too happy when I fired him."

"I wasn't too happy when you fired him. I should have done it and beat the living hell out of him at the same time."

"That wouldn't help, Sam."

"Something's got to."

She knew that. The last five days had been one crisis after another. Hemming had called her twice, wanting to know if she'd reconsidered his offer. Both times she'd turned him down, but she was aware that she seemed to be making an enemy out of the one man in the valley she couldn't afford to be enemies with.

Then George and Tom had quit two days ago. Technically, harvest end wasn't the worst time to lose employees, but they had been with her for years and left without even giving a reason. That problem had boomeranged when Sam had gone down to the docks to pick up some fill-in help for the fall repair work. The last she knew, she had a good reputation as an employer. No one had given Sam the time of day and her name had suddenly become synonymous with leper. It hurt. She had no explanation for it.

She rubbed two fingers to her temples and then pulled herself together. One problem at a time. As far as the vandalism on her truck, her first thought was to call the local sheriff. She hesitated, though. Nat Hemming had the same as gotten Sheriff Lanker elected, and she'd just feel easier if Hemming was unaware she was having problems. "Is the truck fixable?"

"The engine's blown," Sam said bluntly. "You got two choices—to buy a new one, or see if I can pick up an old one at the junkyard."

"Did you find anything else taken, broken, stolen...?"

"Nothing that I've found yet." Sam shifted his weight. "I heard Simon waters down at Harley's bar, like most of the other river rats."

She leveled him a look. "Stay away from there, Sam."

"I never said I was going anywhere near there."

"You didn't have to." She slipped her hands in her back pockets. "I need you to finish up in the lab before you tackle the truck. Do whatever you think is best as far as the engine. You know where the business checkbook is."

"You going out on the river with him again?" Sam motioned toward the lab.

"Yes." She watched a mask drop down over Sam's face and felt a familiar sense of frustration. Both Sam and Mattie had been told that she was simply doing some private work for Nick. Mattie had never questioned that, any more than she'd questioned a few years back when Laura had let a university biology professor trail her around for a few weeks. Sam, though, never liked strangers on the property. His distrust of Nick might have been alleviated if she explained the whole truth of the project, but she couldn't do that to Nick.

She'd also known for a long time that Sam's loyalty to her had a possessive streak. She'd hired him when he was down and out, with a long record of trouble and a mile-wide chip on his shoulder. She must have asked herself a dozen times why she'd taken on a man that no one else would hire, but the answer had never been very complicated. At the time, her own life had been bogged down with the same hopelessness she'd recognized in Sam. He'd paid her back a thousand times for trusting him.

With a troubled expression on her face, she watched him stalk off for the yard. Sam was the least of her worries. For one short second, she was aware that her pulse was frantic, that her mouth tasted of tin. One vandalized truck wasn't the end of the world. Neither was losing a few employees. Only so much seemed to be going wrong so fast and it was terribly important that Nick never discover anything was amiss.

If her troubles came to a point where she felt her ability to protect his formula was jeopardized, she would willingly and honestly tell Nick. Nothing could be allowed to endanger his pearls, but that was part of the problem. He hadn't mentioned it for the last five days, but she hadn't forgotten how easily he had talked about destroying his nutrient formula. She wasn't about to do anything to give him an excuse to bring up the idea again, and they were nearly done with the project now. Hours away from completing his work. In days he'd be gone from her life.

Bittersweet pain washed through her. Avoiding his touch over the last few days had been like walking a tightrope. He made no secret that he wanted her, and the tightrope was of her own making. There could be no physical relationship, but blindly, foolishly she couldn't let go of what she felt. With Nick, she felt special, whole, needed as a woman, so rich, so full ... and so scared.

Inside and out, the emotion of fear had dominated her life this last week. For the first time, she was beginning to question what she could handle, what she couldn't. You can handle what you have to, Laura. You always have, she reminded herself.

She strode toward the lab. A smile was braced on her face even before she turned the doorknob. "Sorry to take so long. Ready to work?" she asked Nick cheerfully.

"Sure." Nick set down his coffee mug and let his eyes roam, slowly, over her suddenly pale features. "You and Sam run into some problems over the workday?"

"Not at all. He just wanted to run through a few details in the work schedule we hadn't covered yesterday."

Her gaze met his squarely and her smile was secure. She fibbed beautifully.

Nick thought fleetingly that he'd never seen her break. He'd envisioned what would happen when the stress built up to an explosion point inside of her.

At that exact moment, he knew he intended to be there, not just to soothe and comfort, but to tackle her damn dragons for her. He reminded himself that in another day he'd have her alone in New York, away from here.

It wasn't soon enough.

Every muscle and bone ached as Nick strode toward the ramshackle bungalow. The princess might be capable of scooping stamina out of thin air, but after a twelve hour workday he craved nothing more than the nearest mattress. The end of their pearl harvest was the last thing on his mind.

The night was pitch-black and chilly. His fingers curled on a brown paper bag, Nick approached a lightless porch, noting curtainless windows, peeling paint and a yard that had long gone to seed. He knocked on a screen door that had a hinge missing. Inside, a TV blared and he had a short glimpse of two faded vinyl chairs before the door creaked open.

Sam stood in the doorway, for a moment neither wary nor hostile—he was too startled at his unexpected visitor. Nick pressed his advantage by stepping in and taking the bottle from the bag. "Moonshine," he said casually. "The best of the local illegal brews, I've been told. Have you got an hour to kill?"

Nick left at three a.m., cold sober. Sam was comfortably passed out, boots removed and a blanket over him, on the ratty couch in his living room.

All Nick could think of was the plane flights confirmed for two, Nashville to New York, leaving at three the next day.

* * *

I don't believe I'm doing this, Laura thought as she plopped four quarters in a slot, pulled the silver knob and watched a minuscule pack of chocolate candies skid to the bottom of the vending machine.

The last time she'd been to an airport, vending machines had produced twice the product for half the price. How old had she been? Twelve, when she'd visited her mother's maiden aunt?

Tugging the bag open, she popped two green candies and headed back for Nick, too aware of the years that had passed since she'd traveled. When she was a kid, people had dressed more formally for plane trips, which was why she was wearing a yellow wool suit, ruffled white blouse and bone pumps. The crowd milling through the terminal was dressed in slacks or jeans, sweaters or sweatshirts. Nick was wearing a red crewneck and dark slacks.

She felt like a red herring in a can of white ones, and all her confidence seemed to be stashed in Silverwater.

Rationally, there was no reason for her not to feel confident. She'd made the hotel reservations and she'd made the appointments with the two pearl dealers, including Saul. Nick had never had to talk her into making this trip with him. She was the one who knew pearls, and she knew how nip and tuck he felt about the future of his nutrient formula. Nothing could be allowed to go wrong, not now, not when they'd come so far. She'd have fought tooth and nail to make this trip with him if she'd had to.

Nick's eyes found hers over a dozen heads as he walked away from the reservations counter, and again her confidence scattered like dust in the wind. She felt inadequate and nervous, overdressed and thoroughly aware that she had no business taking a trip with any man alone. Much less this one who was bearing down on her with a lazy sexy smile and hair still disheveled from their race in from the wind.

Nick looked . . . primitive. No one else seemed to notice and people certainly walked blithely past him. But Laura knew there was an uncivilized streak in that man. She'd seen that determination in his eyes before—the glint of wildness, the sheen of a dare. . . .

He reached down and plucked the bag of candy from her hands. Spilling a handful in his palm, he sorted through for color. "I'm warning you, Laura. If you've eaten all the green ones . . ."

She raised her eyes to the ceiling. *Perhaps, Laura, you might consider relaxing.* "Everyone knows the brown ones taste the same as all the other colors," she said. "Don't you dare touch the orange ones!"

"You've eaten all the green," he accused her.

"There were only three. Is our flight on time?" she asked, changing the subject.

"Yes, and boarding's scheduled in twenty minutes. Do you want to wander or sit?"

"It doesn't matter to me."

"Then we'll wander toward the vending machine."

"You'll need a fortune in quarters," she warned him.

What they needed was a private traffic cop. Hundreds of people spilled at once through the boarding gates. Exuberant little ones and crying babies, executives wielding their briefcases like weapons and droopy-hatted grandmas. So many strangers. A girl in red flew toward a sailor exiting a plane, both so young, eyes only for each other; his hat flew off when he whirled her in a circle.

Emotion, commotion, excitement, expectations. Laura could feel the airport mood catching and tried to dampen it. She should be worrying about the serious problems she'd left at home, concentrating on the business of Nick's pearls. She should be doing just about anything but allowing her heart to thump as hard as a kid's on Christmas morning. One more day. I've got one more day with him, she thought before telling herself, Dammit, Laura, stop it.

"I told you our appointment with Saul Rothburn was for tomorrow afternoon at three?"

Nick didn't answer. He probably couldn't hear her. The noise level was high and too many people kept brushing by them. There was no point in trying to talk, but suddenly she couldn't stop. "I don't personally know Louis Kneberg, but his credentials as an international pearl dealer are as good as Saul's."

When Nick abruptly stopped and firmly clasped her wrist, she really wasn't paying any attention. "There's no need for you to worry about anything. I'll handle both of them, and I deliberately didn't tell them how special these pearls are. I didn't want—"

Even when he moved in front of her instead of beside her, she thought it was because he was protecting her from people traffic. Even when his knuckles gently cocked her chin up. Doggedly, she kept talking.

"You know I trust Saul, but I want you to have at least a second opinion, Nick. I've always worked with Saul because he was a friend of the family; he handled my first pearls, flew down so I wouldn't have to make the trip to New York, and—"

The words all jumbled in her throat when he bent his head and covered her mouth with his. He wouldn't, announced her brain soothingly. Not in a crowd. Nick would never, could never...

It seemed he would. Noise blurred all around her. Loudspeakers announced flights over the rise and fall of strangers' voices. She could feel the slight pinch in her right toe from the heels she hadn't worn in forever. Real life was still there. It was just...muted, softened, paled.

She'd never had a man look at her like that in her life. His eyes were wild, fierce, naked in intent. His hands slid under her suit jacket and molded her crushing close. She couldn't catch her breath. His tongue curled against hers and her blood heated.

She strained for sanity. A little would be enough. Her purse had dropped beside them. That was a sane thought wasn't it? Feeling her breasts tauten and swell against his chest—that wasn't sane. His hands roamed over her back with possessive intimacy—that wasn't sane. He was boldly aroused. Dammit, the man turned on faster than a firecracker, and his mouth kept rubbing over hers, tasting, teasing. He was trying to drug her with the texture of a tongue and smooth warm lips, and none of it was fair. She'd had no reason to think this was coming, no time to shore up defenses.

He didn't release her until a soft wild sound escaped her throat. He stepped back, only inches, surveying the hectic color in her cheeks and the look in her eyes. Then he bent down, reclaimed her purse from the floor and casually draped an arm on her shoulder. "They've called our flight," he mentioned idly.

Thirty minutes later they were airborne, Laura tucked in the seat by the window, Nick next to her. As fast as the seat belt sign disappeared, the stewardess rolled the drinking cart past them. She heard herself ordering a glass of wine and couldn't imagine why. She didn't want it.

She wanted to not be in love with a man named Nick Langg.

"Laura? Are you cold?"

She shook her head, but he ignored her, reaching up to divert the air blower in the ceiling above them. "I could ask for a blanket," he told her.

But she shook her head again, feeling weary. She *was* chilled, but a simple blanket couldn't help. Nothing was going to take away the scars under her blouse. Nothing could make her as unflawed as his pearls.

She wasn't angry at him for his stolen kiss in the airport; how could she be? Nick wasn't the kind to pursue where he wasn't wanted. She was the one who kept offering him engraved invitations. Every time he touched her, she'd given him proof that she wanted him. Maybe that had been inevitable, because she did. Want him.

The deep black pit she'd dug for herself had no sides, no ladders, no escape hatches. She'd known

better from the beginning, only it had never once occurred to her how disastrously powerful a little thing
like falling in love could be.

Nick shifted. His head tipped back and his eyes
closed. She let her gaze rest possessively on his face,
thinking that even relaxed he never lost a certain
awareness. He expected a fight out of life, and his
striking looks sometimes had an arrogant cast. He'd
won most of those fights, and only when she saw a
certain look in his eyes was she aware that he'd lost
some terribly important ones along the way.

"The nose was broken when I was seven, if that's
what you're staring at." He never opened his eyes.

"I wasn't looking at your nose. I was wondering if
you were responsible for Sam's sore head this morning."

"What made you think I had anything to do with
that?"

"He walked up and talked to you. You couldn't realize what a monumental step that was for Sam. He
keeps completely to himself, never makes friends,
never trusts anyone." She added casually, "Find out
anything you wanted to know?"

Nick opened one eye. "His entire life story. Nothing about you."

But he'd asked about her. And his admitting that
was Nick's style—honesty, with a taste of challenge.
She took a sip from the full glass of wine in front of
her, and glanced at him. His body was totally still. He
was waiting for a reaction from her. Waiting for her to
climb all over him for prying?

She unlatched her seat belt so she could more comfortably curl a leg under her, and then leaned back. "There was never anything you could learn about me from Sam that could possibly matter," she said softly. "We're alike, you and I, Nick. We keep the secrets that matter to ourselves."

"That's the only way anyone can protect themselves in the long run."

"Yes."

"When the chips are really down, there's only one person there. To pretend otherwise might be romantic. But it's not life."

"Yes." She knew he understood. It's part of why she'd trusted him almost from the beginning.

"I've lived on pride even more years than you have, Laura. I know exactly what you do because I've done it. Maybe I even understand more than you know." Gently he laced fingers with her. It wasn't a caress but the simple capture of contact. After a long silence he talked again, and when he did his eyes were still closed, his head again leaned back, and their hands were still hooked together.

He told her about a boy whose parents had been divorced by the time he was born. His mother had died young; his father didn't want him. As a toddler, he was raised by a maternal grandfather outside of San Francisco. That grandfather had lost an arm to the Japanese in World War II and hated anything and everything that had to do with the Japanese. That hatred extended freely to a part Japanese grandson.

"I was an unmanageable little hellion before I was half-grown, Laura, which was when they decided to ship me overseas to my father's family."

His father had remarried someone over the years. He'd never wanted an embarrassing reminder of a short bad marriage, which was all Nick was to him, and his stepmother had lost both of her parents to Americans during the Second World War. There was no space in the house for any part Americans, especially not him. At the time he couldn't speak Japanese. He couldn't begin to cope in school. "I was sixteen when they tossed me on Heroshi like unwanted baggage."

Nick finally opened his eyes and dispassionately viewed the emotion in Laura's. "No," he said quietly. "I'm not telling you any of that to make you feel sorry for me, but to explain. I know about pride, honey. I would have taken love anywhere I could get it when I was a kid—love, attention, anyone who even cared. By the time Heroshi found me, it was too late. I'd sealed all those feelings up tight. I made it my own way and I did it alone. I've never belonged to a country, a person, a place. I don't really have any idea if I could change any of that now."

He released her fingers, and she saw his hand fall to his side. Gold skin, blunt fingernails, strong fingers. "It's not too late," she said softly.

"No? You think about it."

She did. She thought about the crushing life of rejection he'd had as a child and about how desperately he needed someone in his life. Not just someone, she decided, but a woman, the right woman. And she thought about secrets. Nick had revealed his, not by accident. Nothing Nick ever did was by accident. He'd risked his pride to open her doors.

From the window, the lights of New York suddenly rushed to meet her. She had images in her head of a city this size, images of cold hard concrete and crime, of teeming people and the cutthroat madness of Wall Street. Maybe it was like that, but that wasn't what she saw. Millions of sparklers danced in the harbor, and the city was as brilliant as a fairy tale, all mystical color and shimmering brightness. For decades on decades, those lights had welcomed and lured dreamers.

She'd always been a dreamer, no apologies and no excuses. Dreams of pearls had sustained her when nothing else had. There was nothing more fragile than the beauty of a pearl, and that was exactly what drew her. No one knew better than she did how easy it was to destroy the flawless, the fragile.

What Nick wanted and needed was someone to share secrets with. Her secrets were not so sacred. Her physical scars, in any sense, were no worse than his emotional ones. They wouldn't have to matter.

If she hadn't fallen in love with him.

Chapter 7

The strange persistent ringing tried to pierce the darkness. Her hand finally groped out of the warm cocoon of covers to bat the source of the sound. She knocked the receiver from the hook before managing to grab it. "Hello?"

"You didn't seriously plan to sleep in this morning of all mornings, did you?"

Somewhere there was a lamp light switch in the hotel room. If she could just find it. "Sleep in? We don't have our first appointment until three. Nick, it's still dark—"

"It's three minutes after five," he confirmed. "I'll be knocking on your door in twenty minutes. Dress warm."

He hung up. She briefly considered hanging him, period, and then dropped the receiver back on the hook and threw back the covers. Flipping every light switch should have induced a basic wakefulness. It didn't. She tried splashing cold water on her face and brushing her teeth, but then she found herself sleepily staring at the sign pasted on the bathroom mirror. Please Don't Use Any More Water Than You Have To.

The sign had touched her sense of humor ever since she saw it. Somehow it was darned hard to be intimidated by the glamor of a city that had a water crisis.

Yawning, she headed for her suitcase, specifically for stockings, a rose skirt and a paisley silk blouse in rose and pale blue that buttoned up the back. The room around her was distinctly disorienting. Lamps hazed a glow on the peach chair and matching bedspread. The blond furniture was nice but old. Between a small table and the bureau and the bed, there wasn't a lot of turning space. Like the sign in the bathroom, somehow she'd expected something different from a New York hotel room near the World Trade Center.

Neon lights? Satin bedsheets? Your small town naiveté is showing, Laura. And it had probably shown to Nick when they'd checked in the night before. She'd expected a key. She'd gotten a piece of white rectangle that slipped into a slot in the door and was thrown out when each hotel guest left. Later, a concierge had knocked at her door to make sure she was settled. Until then Laura had thought concierges were something that popped occasionally into French novels.

Nick had undoubtedly sicked the lady on her. From the moment they'd landed Nick had been behaving differently than she'd expected. By the time they'd left the airport, battled a bewildering choice of transportation through an insanely noisy city, stopped to eat somewhere and checked in at the hotel, it had been past nine. He'd insisted on walking her to her room, on seeing that the silly piece of rectangle fit, and for a space of a second she'd waited, as tense as any president when the red phone rang. Then he'd smiled a devil's smile, and strode down the hall toward his own room. How was she supposed to sleep after that? This was an ungodly hour of the morning, she thought as she pulled on a pale blue corduroy jacket, slipped into navy pumps and a put on her watch, noting with alarm that she only had three minutes to go. Her hairbrush had completely disappeared.

The brush was lying in plain sight next to the bathroom sink. She grabbed it, and brushed her hair at the same time she tried frantically to straighten things—burying her nightgown under the pillow, closing her suitcase, pulling the covers up on her bed.

The knock on the door came too fast. She snatched up her coat and then dropped it. She didn't know if they were going out. She had no idea *what* the man had in mind at five-thirty in the morning.

Nick could have told her what he had in mind at five-thirty in the morning, and at four, three and two. The look of her did nothing to chase the thoughts from his head. She belonged in his bed. Every time he kissed her, she responded like a woman desperate to live, desperate to love. At first glance, he could see her face was still pink from sleep, her eyelids still heavy from dreams. *I could take you so fast you'd never have time to think.*

But that wasn't why he'd wakened her that morning, and he also noticed with a wry grin that she was dressed to have tea with a duchess. "Honey, we need junk clothes, something warm," he scolded softly.

"We do?"

"We do."

She shook her head. "Nick, I didn't pack jeans. I just packed what I thought we'd need for business appointments and maybe a dinner."

"Did you at least bring other shoes?"

"Shoes?" She looked down at her feet. The navy pumps were her best. She didn't mean to keep parroting him but she felt slightly off kilter. Next to his jeans and bulky fisherman sweater she felt dismally overdressed—again—but more than that, Nick was different than he was at home. Soft shadows darkened his eyes; his hair was still damp from a shower. He moved with earthy sensuality, a laziness she'd never seen in him. And the hunger in his eyes was as bold as . . . desire.

"Flat shoes?" he prodded her.

Her leather clogs were a disgrace, just something she'd wandered around in at home rather than be barefoot. She'd slipped them in her suitcase in lieu of slippers, but she certainly never intended to wear them in public.

"Perfect," he announced, but his forehead puckered in a frown as he glanced around. "Why is it that your room is half the size of mine?"

"Because I made the hotel reservations." She'd done that at his expense. She hadn't argued about those expenses—ethically they were only here for the

business of his pearls. Logically, though, Nick was
probably used to traveling in style, whereas she didn't
need more than a bed and a pillow to be content.
"There's nothing wrong with this room, and I'm not
here to throw away your money," she defended.

"You wouldn't know how to do that if you had lessons. And next time, I make the room reservations."

Next time? Her eyes whipped up to his, then lowered. Very obviously there would be no next time. She
changed her shoes while he held her coat. He seemed
to be in a terrible hurry to get out of her room. Where
was the parade? "What on earth do you think we're
going to find to do at five o'clock in the morning?"
she asked delicately.

"See New York."

She arched a brow. "You mean sightsee?"

"God, no." He looked horrified. "I mean see New
York. When was the last time you played?"

It started with a singing cab driver who thought he
could do arias and a mercifully brief ride that dumped
them off in the middle of enchantment. Local resi-
dents didn't seem to understand that most people in
other parts of the country were asleep at five in the
morning. She didn't know the name of the street where
they started walking, but the cab left them off in front
of a street wagon that looked like a painted gypsy
caravan. The vendor sold hot bagels, lavished with
dripping cream cheese.

"Bagels are sold," Nick told her through munched
bites, "anywhere in the world. Baghdad, Kyoto, San
Francisco, every breakfast diner from here to hell. But
they don't taste like this."

She couldn't help looking amused. He dragged a heavy arm around her shoulder.

"I can tell you don't take your bagels seriously, Laura."

"I'm sorry. I've always sort of been the English muffin type myself."

"Anyone can change if given proper motivation," he said sternly.

"I don't argue with anyone at five o'clock in the morning and this is delicious, besides." She craned her neck trying to see a street sign. "Just out of curiosity, do you have the slightest idea where we are?"

"In the middle of life."

That's exactly what she saw. Life. Five lanes of traffic that never unclogged, horns that never stopped honking, busloads of faces. They passed a fat old man arranging oranges for a street display, a bag lady wreathed in rags and carrying a grocery cart, a St. Bernard watching traffic, a couple with matched orange hair. Dawn tipped over the skyline, and they carried Styrofoam cups of coffee for a time.

They wandered past a store window advertising Indian love potions, skirted around a mother wheeling triplets and paused in mutual admiration for a woman wearing gold lamé, negligently trailing a black velvet cape on the street behind her. The changing smells fascinated Laura. Choking exhaust blended with exotic perfumes; vendors hawked fresh oranges and bananas and apples. She could smell newspaper smells and construction smells and marvelous scents drifting out of a place that sold herbal soaps. Street followed street, every one of them a risk of certain death to cross. Taxi drivers seemed to consider it a personal obligation to ignore red lights...and she and Nick kept sneaking smiles at each other.

How could she not smile? Nick was right. They were in the middle of life. The noise and scents and textures and sights were completely different from her sheltered corner of Tennessee. And the excitement was everywhere. They couldn't walk for a block without hearing someone swearing at someone. Husbands discussed divorces with their wives in full view of everyone. Mothers scolded children. Politics were argued and settled between strangers, loudly. The people were like a tide, rolling forward, always fast, immutable.

Nick found her a vendor that sold English muffins. He forced two on her, then purchased giant red apples from another vendor. She didn't know how many streets they'd crossed by then, but she was still munching on the apple when he directed her toward a row of jewelers. One window held a tiara in rubies and diamonds. A second promoted sapphires, and the emeralds in the third window caught her breath.

Nick shook his head. "Not for you, Maybelle." He faked a Tennessee twang.

She matched it. "But Hiram, you promised me a little bauble if the corn came in—"

His laughter was husky and easy. "You can have a million little baubles, Maybelle. But not those. Something that suits you."

Two jewelry shops down he finally found the baubles that "suited" her: a triple strand of pale blue pearls, impossibly rare, fastened with a sapphire clasp and presented on red velvet. Nick leaned up against the brick storefront, watching Laura study those pearls, and something in his easy smile slipped. "Would you like them?" he asked her.

She forced her eyes away from that window and grinned. "I hate to tell you this, Hiram, but the whole state of Iowa doesn't have enough corn to pay for those. Simple diamonds would be a ton cheaper."

"Laura."

She looked up again.

"Honey, do you want them?"

There was such fire in his eyes that her heart stopped. He meant it, and for a minute she didn't know what to do, what to say. His jacket was open, his throat bare to the cold wind. His cheeks had that burn of cold and those eyes of his were so dark, so black.

"I want to buy them for you, Laura," he repeated quietly.

"I want..." But for that instant she didn't know what she wanted. The right to straighten his wind-rumpled hair. It would have been enough.

She settled for a relish-dripping hot dog at eleven o'clock, which she ate while sitting in Central Park and watching a three-man jazz combo practice in the cold wind. Later they spent an hour silently studying paintings in an art museum. After the museum she hooked her arm through his while they watched a street mime show.

By one-thirty, every muscle in her thighs and calves was creaking. Her heel had a blister, and she knew that one stolen day in New York was never going to be enough to share what she wanted and needed with a man she loved.

"Laura, how good to see you!"

"Saul." Laura pressed a kiss to both his cheeks, European style. Saul Rothburn was no taller than she, but he was significantly rounder. The buttons on his white shirt started straining around mid rib and he wore his belt beneath the comfortable bulge. Tufty sprigs of gray hair fuzzed around his ears; there wasn't much on top. Wizened smile lines could have made a stranger judge him as no more than a kindly old man, but Saul's eyes were cool blue and fox-shrewd. His gaze fastened on Nick even before she stepped back. "Nick Langg, Saul. You've met before, I understand."

"Nick." Saul extended a pudgy hand. "I believe I classified you as a rather determined man the first time we met, but I'm willing to forgive you that now. First, because you've had the good sense to bring my Laura to New York, and second because you've had the even better sense to bring me your pearls. You did bring them?"

"Yes."

"So I will find you both a chair, a little coffee. Laura, you look radiantly beautiful, as always. Perfect skin for pearls, I've told you a hundred times. Nick, you are showing my best girl the city?"

Saul kept up a steady patter of conversation as he shifted chairs and found coffee mugs. Downstairs, plush carpeting and discreet lighting provided an elegant setting for a person to be coaxed into buying some of the most expensive jewels on Fifth Avenue. Saul's office, not surprisingly to Laura, was a different kettle of fish. His desk was old, the floor linoleum, and his work space cluttered with the tools of his trade.

As soon as Nick yielded the two drawstring bags of pearls, Saul urged, "So, sit down, both of you. This will take a little time."

Laura firmly shook her head. "I'll watch, Saul."

"You don't trust me?" The little man looked wounded.

"I wouldn't trust God with these pearls. You'll see."

He chuckled, and wasted one more minute bussing her cheek. "I love you, Laura. I've always loved you, from the time I knew your parents, and you were in diapers. I watched you grow up, and keep wondering why I've wasted being married forty years to the wrong woman. Now let me see, let me see."

Gently, gently he poured Nick's pearls on a long square of velvet. Nick could feel the tension build in Laura and he had no illusions that either she or Saul cared if he was there. Birds of a feather, the two only had one thing on their minds. The casual banter was all done and he felt pride rising for Laura. She so obviously knew what she was doing, and Mr. Rothburn was nobody's buddy where his business was concerned.

"Laura, I do not handle dyed pearls. Sweetheart, you knew this."

"They're not dyed."

"If you'd explained to me that they were Tahitian or from Central America—"

"They're from the valley, Saul."

"They're black. They cannot be from your valley. Well . . ." He sighed disparagingly. "I will still look." Slowly he adjusted the spectroscope and loupe over his head. A few minutes later he admitted, "Nominal size," and after what seemed like a year confessed, "I'm not saying I have any quibble with the density."

Laura wasn't sure at what instant she lost patience. With a stranger, she might have managed to simply watch and remain uninvolved, but this was Saul. At some point she shifted next to him. As fast as he finished using one tool, she reached for it, ignoring his amused smiles. "Perhaps you would prefer I was not even in the same room? Somehow I had the impression you wanted *me* to appraise these pearls."

"Hush, Saul. I love you, but hush." Her heart was suddenly beating so hard she had the embarrassing fear she was going to hyperventilate.

She knew exactly what Saul was testing for. At home, she had a refractor and loupe and microscope, all of which gave her the capacity to test for density, size, luminescence and flaws. To a point. Her lab equipment didn't extend to Saul's 20x binocular microscope, radiography and an X ray diffracting light.

X ray diffraction was the most complex test, because it showed the internal layers of nacre and the prismatic crystals of aragonite. Saul used that test for proof that the pearls weren't dyed, proof of the depth of luminescence in each pearl and conclusive proof whether a pearl was cultured or natural. Those things Laura already knew. She searched, far more mercilessly than Saul, for flaws. Any flaws.

The silent litany kept pounding in her ears: there had to be flaws. There *had* to be. Nick's pearls were wonderful, she already knew that, but there was really no such thing as perfect pearls. Unflawed beauty really didn't exist; it was just a dream. Maybe for years she'd let that haunting dream go on too long, mean too much, color her life.

Yet unflawed pearl after pearl passed from Saul's hands to hers. A blond man knocked and tried to interrupt once; Saul snapped, "Get the hell out of here," and the man disappeared.

Still another hour passed before Saul eased the black band of the spectroscope over his head, leaned back and looked from Nick to Laura with no expression. "What the hell have you brought me here?" he demanded. Then he just shook his head, rubbing his chin with his fingers at the same time. "Have you shown these to any other dealers?"

"The issue right now is your judgment," Nick said quietly.

"Yes, of course, but first I want you to know there is no need for you to take these pearls to other dealers. Laura knows me; I knew her family long before she ever got seriously involved in the good gems, the good pearls. I would not cheat you." His gaze focused on Nick. "Mr. Langg, I want you to have no doubts about my credentials as a reputable pearl dealer. My reputation—"

Laura interrupted, "Saul, you have three seconds to tell me what I want to hear before I start tearing my hair out."

"So what is it you want to hear?"

"That they're the best damn pearls you've ever seen."

He shrugged. "They're the best damn pearls I've ever seen." He mentioned to Nick, "She is slightly overexcited."

"I am beside myself," Laura corrected with total truthfulness. She cupped the old man's cheeks in her palms and kissed his forehead. "And you can stop trying to talk to just Nick, you wily old coot. They may be his pearls, but I'm the one you're going to be arguing price with, not Nick."

"You are offending me with every word," Saul said sadly. "All these years I have known you, loved you—"

"Tell him what he has, Saul. Give him a figure."

"She was such a nice girl, but she's turned out so aggressive," Saul said despairingly to Nick, and then swift and flat to Laura, "I never said they were worth the kitchen sink."

"No, because they're worth a devil of a lot more than that. Let's have at it and get this done."

From everything Laura had told him, Nick already had a notion what kind of values they were dealing with. He still felt stunned shock echo through him when the jeweler began bargaining at a figure over two hundred-thousand dollars. Shock was not the word when Laura interjected eight hundred-thousand, and all for a few handfuls of beads.

He couldn't take his eyes off Laura. She gave off the heat, the energy, the excitement of an electric storm. Her eyes were like blue flames, her body alive with passion. The old man undoubtedly believed she was arguing about money. Nick could have told him she was fighting for the pearls, and that nothing so minor as a mountain or an earthquake had better stand in her way.

"Six-five and no more, and you know damn well that's fair," Saul finally roared at her.

Her brows raised in sudden smooth, elegant arches. "Why, of course it is, Saul. I knew you'd see reason. But as I also told you, we need to have at least a second appraisal on them."

Saul's eyes riveted to Nick's. "That is completely unnecessary. For that matter, I could have a second appraisal done here if you wish. In that way, they will be secure in my safe. You certainly don't want to be wandering around New York carrying pearls like these."

"No, Saul—"

"Yes." Nick hadn't wanted to interrupt until he had to. Now he stood up, ignoring Laura's restraining hand on his arm. "Saul, we'll leave them with you for safekeeping, and be in touch with you tomorrow as far as what we want to do with them."

"Fine. An excellent decision," Saul said swiftly. "You will want a receipt and I would feel more comfortable if you actually saw the security measures I have to protect your pearls."

They didn't escape from the jeweler's until after five. By then, occasional specks of snow were drifting down from a steadily darkening sky and the evening had turned bone cold. Every taxi that passed was occupied, and Nick could see Laura shivering like mad—

but not from cold. She also hadn't once stopped talking since they'd left Saul Rothburn's sight.

"You heard? You heard what he said? But Nick, I can't imagine what you were thinking of, leaving them with him. We're going to need them tomorrow for the second appraisal and did you see how he looked at them? Did you actually see? Greed, Nick. Greed was *dripping* from his eyes. Now you understand. Now you have to understand what you have! And that was just one small experiment, nothing next to what we'll do next time. I knew once you really understood that you'd see they were worth any risks; they're worth *everything*, Nick. But I think I could have argued more money with him. I don't think it was enough; I didn't handle it at all well."

She was dancing—her fingers, her eyes, her toes, her lips. She couldn't stand still even when he gently clamped both hands on her shoulders to gain her attention. "You handled it beautifully," he told her. "No one could have done it better."

"You're prejudiced," she accused him fretfully.

"Slightly." He smiled.

"Maybe we should have had a lawyer handle it, Nick. Maybe someone else could have bargained a better price for you—"

"I wanted no one else there but you." Which was true, but guilt razored through him. She'd forgotten—because she didn't want to remember—that he'd never agreed to anything beyond concluding the experiment with an appraisal for the pearls. Only so Laura could have this moment had he allowed the entire project to go this far.

The jeweler's verdict, though, had confirmed every risk he'd been afraid of exposing her to. It mattered to Laura so much that those pearls were perfect. Well, they were, but for Nick that meant that certain decisions could no longer be postponed about her safety and involvement.

It was time to talk, yet the words refused to form. Her eyes had the same brightness and sparkle as the snowflakes. Excitement colored her cheeks; her lips were red, wet. He couldn't take his eyes from her mouth, and he simply couldn't burst her bubble. Not now.

"I keep getting the small feeling you think we have some reason to celebrate?" he asked dryly.

"God, yes." Laughter shimmered from her lips. "This is one night I'll be glad to spend your money. We need a dozen magnums of champagne. The best prime rib in town. Or lobster? I haven't had lobster in years; I love it and... Nick!" She saw his soft smile, but there was worry in his eyes instead of happiness, and here the whole sky was full of rainbows. There was no way she could have stopped herself from throwing her arms around him and squeezing tight. "I swear I could dance on a cloud!"

He held her achingly close and brushed his lips to her forehead, but despair riveted through him. He knew what he wanted and even intended to happen this evening, but he was also aware that their time together was running short. Always the pearls. Always for the pearls she came alive. He'd never had anything to offer that could compare.

If Laura had heard what he was thinking, she could have told him he was wrong. She, too, had plans for the evening that had nothing to do with pearls and that he couldn't possibly anticipate. She had to pray they would go perfectly because the stakes were as high as she'd ever played.

The restaurant was all rich reds and blacks with secluded lighting and discreet waiters and a gold-rimmed menu that listed no prices. The singer was backed by a bassist and piano player; all three knew what to do with a love song. Dinner was excellent, judging from the monumental amount Laura had devoured. Nick couldn't remember a thing he'd eaten and had no idea what song was being played.

After her first glass of champagne, she'd slipped off her shoes under the table. She still wasn't wearing them. When they danced she reached the tip of his chin, and he kept telling himself that she didn't realize what she was doing.

Nothing specific was different about her looks. She'd worn her hair simply brushed back from the crown although she wore a different scent, something that reminded him of white camellias. She was wearing a black velvet skirt and a white blouse—he'd discovered a long time ago that nothing about Laura's blouses qualified exactly as simple. This one was white satin; its collar tipped to points at her throat and wrists. Its back had a million satin buttons, so tiny that he couldn't imagine how she'd managed to do them all up alone.

He kept thinking about those buttons because it was wisest not to think about the way the white satin draped and shadowed her breasts in front. She'd neglected to wear a bra. Several times over the last two hours he'd reminded himself that Laura wasn't the kind of women to ever neglect a bra.

Until that night, though, Laura had never deliberately, provocatively, determinedly tried to drive him over the edge of sanity.

Her thighs courted contact as she moved in rhythm to the dance. The tips of her breasts rubbed with reckless abandon against his chest. Her arms were wound around his neck and her fingers kept sneaking up into his hair. She suddenly tilted her face up, her lips too vulnerably parted, her eyes shining too hard with happiness. "You're not getting tired, are you?"

"You're the one that should be."

"I'm not. I could dance like this forever."

"We're never going home," he agreed, and knew exactly what an illogical, irrational thing that was to say. He let his thumb brush her cheek. She nudged her cheek into his palm. She shouldn't have done that, because he suddenly couldn't breathe.

"I should go put on my shoes. It was all that walking today."

"No one's looking and you don't need your shoes, but if your feet are sore—"

"They're not. They're not," she insisted.

He knew they were, and he kept telling himself that she didn't know what she was doing. She wasn't used to the wine, she was high on the good news about the pearls, and he insisted to himself that he knew her too well to accuse her of teasing a man.

That's exactly what she was doing, though. Those slim little fingers that kept playing with his hair were going to cause him a heart attack. When she nuzzled her cheek into his shoulder, he felt the shudder of stark heat sizzle through him. The brush of her breasts was more than the natural contact of dancing, and her hips were well aware of his arousal. Those hips had rubbed and withdrew, rubbed and withdrew, until he'd become familiar with torture. Want had become craving. Basic desire had become an explosion of need.

"Nick?"

He bent his head to hear her and at the same time she went up on tiptoe. Fire raged through him when her lips reached for his. Never once had he thought of Laura as reckless. Proud, beautiful, capable, and occasionally headstrong, but never reckless.

She took his mouth, a very different experience than all the times he'd taken hers. She was suddenly so serious. Carefully, she used her lips to explore the texture and shape of his, to taste, to woo, to learn. They kissed again, this time with much more courage. Her breath whispered between them, uneven, incomparably sweet. On tiptoe, her body suddenly went still and balancing against him, she tried her tongue.

One of them had to keep some contact with reality. Nick decided it had to be her.

He slid his arms around her shoulders to shield her from anyone's view, and then he made love to her mouth exactly as he wanted to make love to Laura.

A thousand times he'd tried to understand his feelings for her. He knew he felt craving, fascination, frustration, tenderness, desire, protectiveness. He couldn't think of anything he wasn't willing to do to keep her safe or of anyone he wasn't willing to kill who would dare hurt her. She warmed him as no woman ever had. She exposed the hollow loneliness he'd made of his life in the most painful way. Love...he never used the word, mistrusted it, was afraid he was incapable of it. He had no single word to pin down his feelings for Laura.

All he knew was that what he felt for her rocked his world. The control he'd fiercely valued all his life was shattering, piece by piece. "Laura." He had to twist his mouth away from her. "We're going back to the hotel. Now."

"Yes," she whispered.

Chapter 8

Snow pelted down in a fury of white as the cab pulled up to the hotel. Nick paid the driver and climbed out first. Then he grabbed Laura's arm. Ignoring the uniformed doorman, he propelled her through the far entrance and into the closest open elevator.

The snow, a blinding cold wind and all the noises of a restless city at night abruptly ceased. The elevator doors had barely slid shut before Nick leaned back and gathered her to him. Her neck tipped back under the pressure of his kiss and her lips ached before he finally raised his head. Palms framing her face, his eyes searched hers.

If he was looking for proof of her arousal, he could have checked knocking knees and failing lungs. And she had invented a new proverb: intelligent women didn't unleash panthers. She already knew she'd crossed an invisible line in the restaurant. She was aware of exactly what level of danger she'd invited.

Nick wasn't exactly acting like Nick. The fluorescent light illuminated the rigid line of his mouth, the harsh intensity of his features, the black glow in his eyes. Tension crackled from him. So did a primitive heat, even if his hair was still damp from glistening snow.

The elevator's bell tone had barely announced their arrival on the seventh floor before he'd locked his hand with hers. The napped carpet absorbed their footsteps as they traveled the narrow corridor. Her room came first, but when his pace slowed near her door she shook her head. She didn't want to be in her room; she wanted to be in his.

Mr. Langg didn't seem to care where they were as long as they got there, soon. He never released her hand until they arrived at his room and he had to reach in his coat pocket for the rectangular key. The door popped open on a dark room. She was desperately trying to remember how to breathe when she suddenly didn't need to. After all that wild rush Nick took root in the hall. Gently, softly, his knuckles brushed her chin and his tenor was soothing and low. "Your eyes are so huge, and you think I didn't notice how cold your fingers were? Laura, nothing's going to happen that you don't want to happen."

"I know."

"I would never hurt you."

"I know."

"There's nothing you have to be afraid of with me. Nothing. Ever."

"I know." Such fibs. She knew nothing at all, and emotions of panic and anxiety and inadequacy were trying to scissor her nerves into ribbons. She had to move now or risk losing all her courage. She stepped in the room ahead of him, slipping off both her shoes and coat at the same time.

His room would have been pitch-black if he hadn't left the draperies open earlier. The wink of city lights from the window softened the darkness and made it possible for her to make out the shadowed outlines of the bed, dresser, and chairs. Then she heard the door latch behind her, sealing the rest of the world out, as she swallowed one last desperate gulp of oxygen.

Without taking off his coat, Nick moved toward the lamp near the bed. She diverted him by simply touching his wrist. He straightened as if she'd branded him.

Now. It had to be now, before Nick had a chance to think, before he had the chance to catch the rein on his emotions. Her nervousness was suddenly a luxury she had no time for.

While he was standing still, she gently pushed the coat from his shoulders. The fabric was cold, but Nick wasn't. When her fingers slid to his chest, she could feel the heat of his body soar in reaction to her touch.

Cold shadows of fear were trying to jump at her from the corners of the room. She had to do this right and she didn't know how. Her fingers tentatively stroked his ribs, then his sinewed chest through his shirt. He didn't move.

She moved one step closer, willing the heat of him to transfer to some part of her, any part of her. She wasn't sure where the chills were coming from, but she felt numbingly cold, and she could taste copper in her mouth when she loosened the top button of his shirt. He still didn't move. She freed another button and then a third. She thought, Nick, you could help me a great deal if I knew exactly how long you planned to stand there like a rock. What happened to the blood-tingling rush? I could have sworn you were a hair's breadth away from taking me in the elevator. But they weren't in the elevator now, and she'd never lain with a man. Was she doing it all wrong? Did he see her as wanton? Too bold? Maybe he hated assertive lovers. Maybe she was completely turning him off.

Her fingers were shaking so hard she could hardly manage the fourth button. Her knees were like noodles. She told herself that any normal woman doing what she was doing would have her mind on sex. She seemed to have left all her hormones sleeping in Tennessee. The last thing in her mind was sex.

The only thing in her head was love. This man had changed her life. She'd never thought of her pearls as a way to hide from life, but that had always been what she was doing. Pretending she could escape feeling a woman's needs, a woman's wants. Pretending her pearls could erase loneliness. In one portion of her heart, she fiercely resented Nick for shattering illusions that had kept her safe for eight long years.

All she wanted to do this night was shatter a few of his. Nick wasn't alone. From this night on, anywhere he went, anywhere he lived, no matter what he did, she wanted him to understand that there was a woman who loved him. He'd never have that right to be completely alone again.

A future? They didn't have one. No shared promises, not even time, and Laura very definitely hadn't forgotten her scars. She had nothing to give Nick but one time, one sampling of the woman she was and wanted to be, and maybe that was exactly where her courage came from.

Weariness and wine flavored her recklessness. She suddenly understood his total stillness. Control. He was fighting like hell for it.

You sweetheart. You can have everything, Nick, don't you understand? Everything but control.

Pushing that control of his proved not so difficult. Curiosity seemed to come with loving him. She wanted to know what would happen if her lips skidded across his bare chest. Pushing off his shirt, she found out. She wanted to know what would happen when she rubbed satin against his bareness. She found that out, too.

Her tongue played in the hollow of his shoulder. Her palms, flat, snaked down his lean sides to his hips, and she sensed more than saw the instant that Nick came completely apart.

His groan was half a whispered roar when his mouth slammed on hers. She might have laughed from sheer joy if she could have breathed. She couldn't. He lifted her and came back down with her on the scratchy bedspread. Limbs tangled, he never severed that kiss, and everything she was afraid would be hard was so easy.

She didn't need experience to know what he wanted. His mouth was hungry; her lips nourished him. He needed to be touched and loved; she touched and loved him. His skin needed the covering of hands in the cold darkness. The grain of his beard needed to be stroked. The rough thick texture of his hair needed fingers in it.

The man needed a woman's limbs wrapped around him, tight, warm, protective. He needed protecting, her Nick. Tonight she could take on the shadows of the lonely boy traveling oceans to find a place he belonged, the too strong man too proud to walk in anyone's shadow. She could protect him from anything.

She heard his shoes drop to the floor. In the darkness his hands were everywhere at once. It was an impossible feat, but there was a time to worry about reality and a time to savor magic. He had palms to cover her breasts until their tips strained their satin sheath, to thread through her hair, to touch her spine and her hips and glide down her thighs. He had the most dangerous hands she'd ever imagined...but never more dangerous than when he suddenly shifted. His weight pinned her flat to the bed and his fingers gently clamped on both her wrists.

Darkness had turned smoke-gray. She could see the outline of his face; the ink sheen in his eyes hovered above her. He was having a terrible time trying to breathe.

"I've thought of you too many times like this. Wild and willing, all beauty and fire." He shook his head once, blindly. "Laura, you have to understand how little control I have. If you're not absolutely sure you want this, you've got to tell me now."

"I'm very sure." She cradled his face with her palms. She'd misjudged this moment. She should have known that through heaven and hell, earthquakes and gales, Nick would find some way to do the honorable thing. Shudders were still racking through him and the bones in his face could have been carved in marble.

"Laura?" She didn't want to talk anymore, yet insistent, swift, his lips claimed hers and then lifted. "Are you innocent?"

She hadn't expected the question and felt a surge of alarm that he'd even asked it. Every instinct warned her that Nick would weigh the wrong answer with honor and responsibility. It would change the way they made love, and she couldn't let that happen.

"Do I strike you as innocent?" she whispered fiercely. "Do I strike you as a woman who doesn't know her own mind, make her own choices, accept her own risks? I know what I want, Nick. I always have, and right now it's you. Now. Inside me."

But it had to be her way, and the fierce, drugging kiss he offered her mouth nearly stole the last of her sanity. She felt his fingers groping for the buttons at the back of her blouse, and she managed to claim his right hand and guide it down to her thigh. Her skirt was already hiked halfway to her waist and beneath that she had stockings. She led his palm to exactly where stockings turned into flesh. The garters were no more than a scrap of lace.

"Unhook them for me," she whispered. "All evening, I've been waiting for you to unhook those stockings for me. To know that I was bare for you underneath it. Don't make me wait any longer, Nick. Don't make me wait...."

On a single thread of a breath she knew she'd tested the last shred of his control, and that she'd won. Despair shimmered through her for the choices she couldn't give him—choices of bareness, of slow sweet lovemaking, of time to explore the tenderness of lovers. But it had to be mindlessly fast. He had to be out of control, not thinking but acting only on emotion. Willingly she would abandon everything and all she ..ad for Nick . . . as long as she didn't have to risk his look of revulsion for her scars.

Ugly. Flawed. Scarred. The indelible images burned in her head hauntingly and that pain had never been greater. She wanted to give him something better. Something perfect. Something beautiful. Something that Laura Jakway had lost the capacity to be.

She felt the cool darkness feather over her legs as Nick's palms chased down her stockings. He murmured something, fierce and low. He didn't mean it. She couldn't really make him feel that way. Yet the despair slipping into her mood fragmented, disappeared, as she understood the reality of Nick as a lover. When he slipped the skirt down over her hips, she reached for the belt at his waist, but he moved faster.

He stood for a minute to remove the last of his clothes, and when he came back down to her, she was afraid he'd think again about removing her blouse. She gave him other things to worry about. Maybe she'd unleashed the panther in Nick, but he'd released something consumingly powerful in her that she'd never expected.

She was trembling very hard. He had to do something about that. She was beginning to feel dizzy with a need so fierce that the blood was pounding in her ears. He had to do something about that, too.

She needed to touch him all at once, to hold him. There were odd wild sounds whispering from her throat and all the self-control she'd taken for granted was gone.

Nick was supposed to help her, and he was only making it worse. He whispered to her, wild, sinful things. He shouldn't have kissed her...where he kissed her. The moistness between her thighs embarrassed her; her skin was growing slick and damp and there were scents she hadn't expected. Musk. Heat.

She understood the technical details of intimacy. She hadn't understood how smooth and hot and hard his flesh would be, how vibrantly he would react when she touched him. She didn't know the whole world could sizzle. She didn't know how desperately a woman could want. A woman could die like this. Nick didn't seem to care. He seemed to think there was more when it was perfectly obvious there couldn't be more.

But there was. When he knelt over her, she'd never had time to build up fear. That first thrust sent diamonds of pain shimmering through her, and one short explosive breath from Nick.

"Dammit, Laura—"

"No, no. Don't stop." That first pain was quick and sharp, but there followed a completely different kind. The ache was like a rage. She felt invaded, swamped by the total sensation of vulnerability. She'd been hollow until that moment without ever knowing it. She'd been empty all this time, and all men and women had been wrong from the beginning of time. This wasn't possible. She was either too small or he was too large. She was going to tear apart if he moved. She was going to go out of her mind if he didn't. "Don't stop, Nick..."

But his lips suddenly rained soft, slow kisses on her chin, her cheeks, the moistness seeping under eyes. "That's the last lie you'll ever bring to this bed, love."

"Nick—"

"Ssh. I'm not scolding. I'm just angry at myself for believing you, but we're not going to talk about that now. Right now I want you to give me your mouth. And I want you to wrap those long legs of yours as tight around me as you can. And then I'm going to show you exactly how beautiful you are, Laura. I'm going to love you until those blue eyes of yours look wild and lost."

All her adult life she'd been afraid of fire. This wasn't fire as she knew it. This was branding heat and searing brightness. This was wonder. This was a fire of rainbows. Easy, slow, he moved inside of her until she understood the aching discomfort was something good, something natural, something right. Then, lips clinging, limbs tangled, he changed that pulse of rhythm until heat started to rebuild inside her. By the time he caught the fever, she'd already yielded to abandon. There was no choice.

A wild sweet cry escaped her lips, she heard Nick's harsh groan. Then there was only the weight of him, welcomed, warm, and the sound of hoarse breathing in the darkness. Minutes slipped past.

Everything that had ever been complicated in her life was reduced to the simplest proportions. She had no more energy than a sleepy butterfly.

Nick shifted to his side, drawing her with him. Eyes closed, he felt the tickle of her hair against his cheek, the smooth expanse of her bare leg locked between his, the feel of her small hip under his palm.

Fierce possessiveness flooded through him, and a totally alien, shattering sensation of vulnerability as a man. Neither emotion was expected. Neither did he know what to do with.

In time, he found the strength to raise up and turn the lamp on behind her. Laura startled, her eyes blinking open. He paid no attention, too absorbed in studying this woman who'd just rocked his world to kingdom come.

She didn't look like the demanding temptress who'd wantonly teased him into forgetting all the skill, gentleness, tender exploration and sensitivity he'd intended to bring her as a lover.

There was no way she looked like she could have reached the age of twenty-seven without a lover.

Her hair was in wild disarray, her mouth red, and her eyes had the sleepy smudge of exhaustion and satiation. Curled up and small, she looked like a defenseless kitten. Precious. Fragile.

She was still wearing that blouse. An hour before, the erotic rub of satin against his bare skin had driven every thought from his head but taking her. Now, he looked at her and couldn't believe what he'd done.

"Are you all right?" he whispered.

Her lids slid down again. "I haven't any idea. I'm dead and in heaven. Nick?"

He smiled, brushing his lips on her brow. "Hmm?"

"Was it . . . nice for you?"

"No." That sent her lashes sweeping up again. "It wasn't nice. Nice is a word for sunny days and blueberry muffins, and maybe even a word for when two people make love. But not for what just happened between us. I wouldn't trade the earth and stars for what just happened to us, and I have never felt for any woman what I just felt for you. You're a dangerous lover, Laura Jakway."

She couldn't say anything for a minute. It was illusion, she knew, but for that instant she'd never felt more soaring exhilaration as a woman than she'd ever dreamed. "I'm quite positive it was the other way around."

He touched her nose. "I'm afraid you know absolutely nothing," he said regretfully.

"Nick, don't argue with me."

"I'm sorry."

"You should be. Because of you, I may never find the energy to move again."

"Again, I'm sorry."

"You're not the least sorry. You're smiling."

"Because I was thinking about kissing your bare bottom."

"Nick!"

With a chuckle he slowly eased off the bed, padded barefoot to close the drapes and then strode for the bathroom, where he tossed a clean washcloth in the sink and turned on the hot water tap.

She'd eased a pillow behind her and pulled up the covers by the time he returned. "What are you doing?"

Gently he peeled those covers out of her hand. "You should have told me." He didn't make it an accusation, just a simple statement.

Her skin was already flushed, but a new layer of peach crept along the line of her cheekbones. "I know what you thought," she said uncomfortably. "I think you misunderstood innocence for...It had just been so long since I'd been involved with anyone that I..."

He didn't call her on the fib. He simply took the warm damp cloth and brushed it gently between her legs. Foolishly, she tried to clamp her thighs together. "Nick!"

"I could have made it a thousand times better for you if I'd known," he said quietly, and then stood up and took the cloth back to the bathroom.

"Nick?"

He padded back in.

Haltingly, sweetly, she murmured, "You couldn't have made it better. There's no way anything could have been better."

Abruptly the word love invaded Nick's thoughts. The word he disliked so much, because it implied dependency and vulnerability, the word that raised questions he had no answers for, and the emotion he'd denied needing his entire life abruptly swamped him.

Climbing in beside her, he made a point out of straightening the tangled sheets, bedspread and blankets. Three times he interrupted the process to kiss her, once on her toe, once on her knee, and once—just once, because more wasn't safe—on her mouth.

She was half laughing when he tugged her to him, but she stiffened like a railroad tie when his fingers slid from her collarbone to her nape.

"What are you doing?"

"Unbuttoning your blouse, naturally. Obviously you can't sleep in it."

"No, wait—"

He thought he understood her hesitation, and his tone was soothing, light. "I wouldn't make love to you again tonight, Laura. Do you think I'm unaware that you're sore? All I had in mind was holding you, seeing you. Touch. No more." Every one of those million buttons had an intricate latch. He hadn't loosened three before she bolted back against the headboard, anxiety and a sick-glazed look in her eyes that he couldn't begin to understand.

His hands for that second were in midair. Perplexed, he dropped them. "What's wrong?"

"Nothing's wrong." She pushed a hand through her hair, trying to find anything for her eyes to focus on but Nick's. "I have to go. Back to my room."

It would be hours later before he made the association between her bolting and all those high-necked blouses that he'd always assumed were simply a part of Laura. Now the thought never crossed his mind. Acid was too busy burning a hole in his stomach. "You never intended to sleep here?" he asked tightly.

"I don't think it would be a good idea." She leaned forward to climb out of bed. His fingers closed on her wrist.

He loosened his grip the instant he realized he was hurting her, but he didn't let her go. "You don't mean that."

Words tripped off her tongue, all coming from a throat suddenly so dry it was aching. "We both know what happened," she said softly. "We were both excited about your pearls; we'd had a long day and it was a day we finished off with a lot of champagne. I don't regret what happened, Nick, and I'd like to believe that you don't either, but we can't be foolish about this."

"Foolish?"

"You're going to be leaving soon—not just New York, but my life. You have your own business, your own work." She whispered, "Nothing would work long-term. You already knew that."

His conscience was already aware of those complications.

"You needed someone tonight. So did I." Finally, she glanced at him, about the same time he abruptly released her hand. He looked so cold.

She wanted to tell him a dozen things. He had to find a woman who traveled in his world, because she couldn't stand the thought of his being alone. He'd always allowed himself to be lonely for all the wrong reasons and she desperately hoped she'd made a difference in his life. Perhaps what they'd shared had opened emotional doors for him. Only she couldn't say any of those things without revealing how much she cared.

She forced a smile. Her tone experimented with cheerfulness. "Come on, Nick. Everything's fine. We made love, a choice we both wanted. People do it all the time without making it into something more complicated."

When she was finished, he was so furious he couldn't breathe. He didn't know why he was so angry. He didn't care. "And that's all you wanted? One night. No strings, no possibilities, no commitments."

"Of course."

He was slightly inclined to take that "of course" and wrap it around her neck. Her trying to casually expound the virtues of one-night stands was almost as ridiculous as her lie about her virginity.

He felt shaken. The knots tying in his stomach reminded him that he had no rights to Laura. He hadn't any confidence in the fragile emotions swamping him. He needed to have discussed the pearl business with her before this. He needed to know that she wanted him for more than pearls. He wanted the right to share, caretake, protect, make love to, but no man could take those rights. They had to be given.

Laura wanted those doors closed before they were even opened.

An honorable man would care and respect what she wanted.

A growl escaped him and he had no trace of honor. "You're staying here tonight." Blind angry, he flicked off the light next to the bed and then reached for

Laura, dragged her down to the pillow next to him, daring dragons, armies, earthquakes to stop him.

She said nothing as he fitted her hips in the cradle of his thighs. He smoothed back her hair, rearranged the covers to her chin and then slipped his hand back under the sheets, pushing her blouse up so he could drape his arm on her bare abdomen. She made it reasonably easy to accomplish all that because she'd completely stopped breathing.

That made him mad, too. "Try moving," he suggested lowly.

She did move, then. She turned in his arms, slowly in the dark, and he felt her fingers slide to his neck. Her knuckles touched his chin. "I never meant to hurt you," she whispered.

He told himself to quit worrying about that word love. Did it have to matter? As a boy he'd chased the earth for a simple word that people used casually for meringue, new shoes, sunshine. The rage of hurt knifing through him would lessen if he could just keep love out of this. Who was to say he even knew what it meant?

What he knew was that he wanted her next to him, curled up where he could see her, touch her, shield her, smell that perfume of hers, hear her voice. Regularly.

"Are you too cold?" he asked her.

"No."

"Are you too hot?"

"No."

"I want you to sleep."

"I nearly am," she murmured dryly.

He wasn't. Her breathing evened in minutes, and over the long night hours she turned into a sprawler, a blanket thief, and from time to time, a violent snuggler. It was a full-time job just to keep her covered.

What kept Nick awake and glaring at a black ceiling were visions of other men applying for that job.

Chapter 9

Carrying her shoes, Laura slipped out of Nick's room at eight the next morning. She'd left him dead asleep, but she still tiptoed down the hall until she was completely out of earshot, then dropped her pumps to the carpeted corridor and slipped into them. Her mood unsettled and her eyesight foggy, she turned the corner toward her own room.

Three times in the night she'd tried to rise and leave Nick. Three times she simply hadn't. She thought of a million excuses. His arm had been around her, she hadn't wanted to disturb him, the room was too cool, the night too dark.

She'd run out of reasons. One night, she reminded herself. That was what you wanted, Laura. All you wanted, and exactly what you had. So what's your problem now?

Everything. She stopped in front of her room and pushed the clasp on her purse, searching for the white rectangle key. She'd never wanted to lie to him. Her fingers foraged through lipstick, brush, change purse. She'd never wanted to cheapen that one time by making Nick believe she only wanted a quick fling. She fished through old receipts, a small perfume vial, and then, finally, she found the strange hotel key. He'd come too close to discovering her scars. It was only a miracle that he hadn't. Only a fool would have taken all the risks she'd taken.

She stuck the rectangle in the door slot. All of that was the problem, yet none of it was. The overwhelming problem was a woman's greed. *Her* greed. Because one time, one night, was not enough. Making love with him once had sealed love in, not locked it out. He gave so much. He needed so much. He...

She sighed, pushed open the door, and then stopped dead. Shock bolted through her system before the fear set in.

Yesterday afternoon, she'd left a lamp on—not the overhead light. She'd also left a neatly made bed, a closed and locked suitcase, open draperies, a pair of shoes under the dresser and her toiletries neatly stashed in a carryall in the bathroom.

The covers had been torn from the bed, and every drawer had been pulled out. Her locked suitcase had been pried open. Her blouses, the yellow suit, her stockings, even her underwear—everything was slashed and ripped. Even the lining in the suitcase had been shredded.

Nothing had been spared. In the bathroom, her toothpaste tube had been sliced open, her lipstick smashed and her perfume bottle was in splinters on the floor.

The room was so silent she could hear the beat of her heart. Her gaze skimmed from disaster to disaster, yet nothing seemed to register in her head. Obviously this wasn't real. Why on earth would anyone do that to a tube of toothpaste?

She glanced at the band of her gold watch hanging in the open from a dresser top. It was really the only thing of value she'd brought with her. What kind of thief would go to all this trouble and then leave the watch?

She touched her temples with trembling fingers as she realized that absolutely nothing was taken. The room was basically unharmed. Only the things that personally belonged to her had been destroyed, maliciously and deliberately. Not taken. Destroyed.

Fear coiled through her veins like a snake, slow, insidious, immobilizing. It was so ugly. Violence in any form was ugly, but the idea of violence personally directed at her made nausea rise in her throat. Suddenly even the glare of the overhead light seemed threatening. Her gaze riveted to the phone, yet she couldn't force herself to cross the room.

She backed out a step and then another step, and then her heels started clicking, fast and then faster. Room numbers flew past her in the hall, 709, 711, 713, 715. She rapped on Nick's door, and when he didn't immediately answer, she pounded harder.

Pants on but unbuttoned, Nick grabbed the door handle in a fine mood to let the maid have a piece of his mind. The room behind him was still dark because of the closed drapes, his bed was still warm from where he'd leaped from it. Disturbed from sleep, he wasn't awake enough to think. The instant he saw Laura's face he didn't need to.

"Hi. I know you were still sleeping and I'm sorry I woke you, but—"

"What's wrong?"

She certainly intended to tell him rationally. She'd never crumbled in a crisis before, and after last night it was the last thing she wanted to do around Nick. She tried to talk, when huge shudders suddenly racked her body. Her lungs couldn't find any oxygen. It was like someone else had jumped in her body, someone made of ice. She wasn't Laura. Maybe that was the most panicky thing of all.

A passerby hesitated curiously in the doorway. Nick slammed the door closed with his foot, and then gathered her up. "One question and fast. Are you physically hurt?"

"No. No, I—" Some corner of her had kept shouting *there's no excuse for this,* but humiliatingly giant gulps of air kept blocking her throat.

"Okay. Sshh. Sshh. Don't talk. Just relax. Everything's all right." Her arms flailed out; he tucked them around his waist and pressed her cold cheek to his bare chest. Her satin blouse was all rumpled and he rumpled it more by rubbing the warmth from his hands into her shoulders, her back, her neck. He felt the score of her nails on his spine, but all he could think about was warming her.

"I don't know what's the matter with me! I—"

"Ssh." She'd obviously never suffered an anxiety attack before. "You're safe. You're safe, Laura."

"I can't go back in there—"

"You're not going anywhere."

"It wasn't just chance! That's what terrified me. They would have taken the watch if it was just chance. I—"

"Will you hush?" He rubbed, soothed, scolded her. Long seconds passed. Gradually blood started circulating through her body. She stopped shaking so hard; her lungs stopped overdosing on oxygen. At some point she stilled and his heart started working again. Gently he eased just enough distance from her so he could see her face. Her cheeks were still white as snow; her lips were bitten red. Her eyes reflected exhaustion and anxiety and embarrassment and she was trying, fast, to ease away from his arms.

"I feel like..." She still couldn't make her voice sound right. "A total idiot. Lord, Nick, I'm sor—"

"Don't you dare say it." He smoothed back her hair. Questions were snapping through his mind; his whole body was tensed to react to whatever trouble had brought on her anxiety attack. For a long moment, though, he just held her and absorbed a powerfully sweet awareness. She'd come to him. For another woman, it might have been an obviously simple thing to turn to someone else in time of trouble. He knew damn well it wasn't for Laura.

"Darnit, stop smiling, Nick. You don't understand. I have to tell you what happened."

"And right now," he agreed.

His smile didn't last long. By the time he was reaching for the phone to call hotel security, the groove in his forehead was an iron slash. Three people from the hotel management were knocking at the door within five minutes. He'd expected them to make it in three.

Four hours winged by with incomparable speed. He left Laura locked in his room when he went with the hotel people to see hers. Rage hit the fan when he saw what had happened. As Nick could have guessed, insurance covered the hotel's liability. Management was panicked at the thought of publicity after working hard and long to build a sound reputation for tight security for their guests. And they had no answers.

Neither did the police, and Nick knew exactly what would happen to the report they made out. They kept asking idiotic questions about revenge, grudges, personal enemies. Everyone who saw the room concluded that the crime had been intended against Laura specifically, but the bottom lines were brick walls: nothing had been taken; there was no clue to the identity of the vandal; and no motive for anyone to investigate.

Motivation. The word kept ticking through him like a time bomb. His pearls were the obvious motivation, yet barely a handful of people knew they existed, and only one of them in New York—Saul Rothburn. And Saul *had* the pearls.

Nick was alone with Laura when her face suddenly turned white with guilt and horror. She hadn't made the association of his pearls to the break-in until then. Being Laura, she rushed to take responsibility for anything she could have done that could have jeopardized his formula.

Words tumbled out of her mouth about a neighbor of hers, about sugar in her gas tank, about a fired employee. "Maybe I should have told you before, but it never occurred to me. No one at home knows about your pearls, Nick. Lord, I'd have told you immediately if I thought your pearls had anything to do with my business problems. They couldn't. Even now, I can't see any possible relationship between this in New York and anything that happened in Tennessee."

Neither could Nick, but for the first time, he had a measure of the troubles that had been haunting her these past weeks, and he headed for the telephone. He contacted Saul, canceled the appointment with the second appraiser and changed their flight reservations. "Now, just wait a minute," Laura kept saying firmly.

She repeated that phrase often enough while he made a second series of phone calls. He knew she needed a toothbrush and that she also didn't have a damn thing to travel in except the black velvet skirt and wrinkled satin blouse she was wearing. She needed clothes, a shower and food, all of which she denied, and she balked—just like a woman—at telling him her shoe size.

Room service delivered the packages. She was still protesting about leaving when he pulled her into a taxi headed for the airport.

For all the fast pace, the answered questions and problems that seemed to be multiplying out of control, Nick couldn't remember feeling more relaxed. He was well aware Laura thought he was overreacting to the vandalism of her room. Truthfully, he wasn't. He was reacting to needs.

When he'd made love to Laura, he'd met up with his needs—and with an explosion of emotion that had her name at the end of it. When she'd come to him this morning, she'd needed him. Maybe not as much or as deeply as he needed her, but one crossed bridge at a time.

He wasn't leaving her. And that was that.

A long day of nerves was catching up with Laura. The vibration of the jet engines echoed in her stomach. City lights winked and shined through the narrow window and then the jet was up and climbing into a fathomless evening sky.

It seemed they were barely off the ground before the flight attendant, wearing an apron over her uniform, paused in front of them with a dinner cart. "Beef Wellington or Veal Parmigiana?"

Laura shook her head. "Nothing, thank you—"

"Beef for both of us," Nick interjected mildly. "And wine with the dinner for the lady."

The attendant unlatched the trays from the seats in front of them, set down their covered dinners and moved on. "Nick, I am not hungry," Laura told him.

"You thought I was ordering for you? The size of plane servings is so small, I can probably eat yours and mine. Just open it up and take a look," he coaxed.

"I will, but it won't make any difference." She peeled back the tin foil. A muffin was still steaming, braised potatoes had been browned with parsley, and the beef and baby carrots looked fork tender. She fussed with the plastic silverware only to have something to do. When Nick leaned over and lavished honey on her muffin, she said wearily. "I have an announcement to make, Mr. Langg."

"Oh? Just try one small piece of potato."

"I have not metamorphosed into dandelion fluff since this morning." She jammed the potato in her mouth because he was obviously going to patiently hold the fork for the next ten years if she didn't.

"No?"

Parsley and butter and potato started melting on her tongue, oblivious. "I am slightly tired. This has been a horrible day. I was also scared this morning, I admit it, but that does not mean I have suddenly turned into the track for your train."

"Now that you've got that off your chest, try a bite of the beef," he suggested.

"I am not hungry."

"Of course you are. You haven't eaten all day."

She closed her eyes, striving for patience. Next to her, Nick's hair was brushed the way he always brushed it. No one had sneaked in during that long day and changed his coloring or his bone structure. He didn't look unreasonable, caveman-possessive, proprietorial, dictatorial or domineering. There were no physical changes to explain the monster he'd turned into.

How did an extremely tired woman argue with a steamroller? When she opened her eyes, he wasn't happy that she'd devoured the beef. Now he was waving a muffin in front of her nose.

"It's delicious. You won't believe it until you taste it."

She took the muffin and talked slowly and carefully in the vain hope she might dent the brick wall. "Nick, you can't come home with me, and you definitely can't stay at the house. There's no reason for you to. You've blown this all out of proportion."

"You haven't touched your wine."

She took a long painful breath. "Nick, is this about trust? Have you been thinking that I told someone about your pearl project? Because I didn't."

"I never thought you did."

"I would have told you about the problems I was having at home if I'd believed they affected my ability to protect your pearls. I didn't believe that, and I still don't. Before we expand the use of your formula, I'll add completely new security measures, change a great deal about my business...."

"That's one of the things we'll talk about when we get home," Nick agreed. As much as he wanted her to stop worrying about his pearls, he didn't press the subject. Laura was so sure he was coming back with her because of their unfinished business regarding his formula. Believing that for a while longer wouldn't hurt her.

The flight attendant returned to clean up and Nick relatched the trays so they had more legroom. Then he turned his face to Laura.

All he was doing was looking at her, but a weakness started in her toes and it spread from the inside out. All day she'd been trying to forget. She'd had better things to do than remember the precise intimate moment when he'd penetrated her body. She tried to forget the whirlwind of fire in the darkness. But she couldn't put aside the memory of wrapping around him like an abandoned waif and of feeling precious, flawless and more beautiful than ever from her mind.

"Don't," she whispered.

"Don't what?"

"Don't look at me that way."

"Sweetheart," he murmured softly, "you're looking at me exactly the same way."

"I'm not and I can't be." All the gray matter that was supposed to make up her brain was disintegrating.

"One of these days—soon—I'm going to take your favorite word and roast it like a marshmallow."

"Could you be serious for two seconds?"

The devilish gleam in his eyes seemed to suspend, soften. "Can you be?"

"Yes!"

"Then listen," he said quietly, fiercely. "You're proud and you're strong and you're independent, and I love those qualities in you. You've also had a plague of trouble in recent weeks that's scared you. I have no doubt in hell that you can handle it, but I want to help.

Just come that far, Laura. Far enough to admit that you want someone there for you."

"I . . ." She hesitated. "I admit that if the pearl nutrient was mine, I would want the right to be involved in anything that had to do with security—"

Short and low, Nick told her what he thought about that excuse.

"All right," she whispered with exasperation. "I want you there, Nick. I've been scared. I would appreciate your perspective and your judgment, and I'd just like to talk to someone I can trust. Now if that's what you wanted to hear—"

"That's what I wanted to hear."

"But—"

"We'll worry about all the 'buts' when we get home. Not now."

Five days later Laura stood by her kitchen window, one hand on her hip and the other holding a fresh mug of coffee. Her eyes narrowed on the yard.

The fence was handsome as fences went, and in another three days it would completely enclose the land borders of her property. It was a fence she couldn't afford, being put up by a crew she hadn't hired, and the project had been initiated by the same man who had taken great joy in turning her universe topsy-turvy.

The old proverb required a minor adjustment to apply to Nick: Give him an inch and he took over lock, stock and barrel. Beyond the three hours he spent making long-distance phone calls every day, his waking hours concentrated on making changes in her life. More pitiful than that, she was letting him.

She loved that man.

He was also beginning to terrify her. How long was he going to wait before he pressed for a physical relationship again?

How long was she going to allow herself to pretend that Nick was here for his pearls? Every security system he was adopting could be viewed as an effort to secure the long-term future of his pearl formula, and she desperately wanted to grow those pearls for him.

She desperately wanted a lot of things from Nick Langg that she simply couldn't have: the luxury of trust, of having someone to depend on, someone who asked nothing more from her than to simply be there. Eight years of built-up pride seemed to have easily flown out the door. But dammit, her scars hadn't. Could she risk having an entire relationship disintegrate into pity?

No.

A slight frown creased her brow as she saw two pickups drive in the yard. Sam was behind one wheel, Nick behind the other. They both climbed out of the trucks at the same time and strode toward each other.

Sam wiped his brow with his forearm and then threw his head back in laughter in reaction to something Nick said. Never mind that Sam seemed to be sneakily taking side orders from Nick these last few days, she couldn't imagine what the red-roofed contraption in the bed of the first pickup was. She set the coffee cup on the counter and strode for the door.

Both men exchanged glances when they saw Laura flying from the house. Sunlight caught the glint in her eyes and flickered off the autumn-gold of her blouse that matched the color of turning leaves.

For a moment Nick was mesmerized, caught up in the same cobweb of emotion he felt whenever she was near. When they looked at each other, the air sizzled. When he touched her, she withdrew. He could catch need, desire, wistful yearning in her face. But he couldn't catch Laura.

Independence and pride were very much part of her character, but for days now he'd guessed she had fears of another dimension that affected her feelings about a relationship. A man couldn't force trust. He'd backed down, wanting to give her time, and had used these days to help her in different arenas—investigating her dragons, securing her fortress, seeking answers for what had happened to her here and in New York.

Frustration was becoming his best friend. Answers eluded him right and left. He couldn't continue to run his business long-distance forever. Laura knew he was evading questions about their pearl partnership. He was terrified that to press too hard was to lose her.

He couldn't lose her, and he couldn't seem to find the key to help her, which left him in a deep pit. Now his blue-eyed angel was bearing down on him with her hands on her hips.

"What are the two of you doing now?" Laura's voice reeked patience.

Sam exchanged another glance with Nick then patted the back of the truck bed and turned. "I'll go steal three or four men from the fence crew. Give me fifteen minutes or so, and then we'll get this taken care of.''

"What exactly is this that 'we're' taking care of?'' Laura crossed to the side of the truck and peered at the red-roofed structure. It was too small for a storage shed and too big for a dollhouse.

"Now, Laura—''

"It's possible, bridging right up there into probable, that if I hear one more 'Now, Laura' out of either you or Sam or Mattie—''

"I brought you a little present," he interrupted, and with a crooked finger and a grin motioned her to the second pickup. "Except that regrettably one little present seemed to have turned into nine.''

She shook her head. "I don't know what you're up to this time.'' She tried very hard to maintain the severe frown when she leaned over the side of the second truck bed. Until she looked.

The giant brown German Shepherd with her tongue hanging out was lying on a decrepit blanket. Ears pointed to the sky when she saw Laura, and then the tail started thumping. The Shepherd was unquestionably a lady, one who'd gotten herself in a pack of trouble. A pack of eight, actually, and the round furry pups were swarming all over her.

"Now, I know she doesn't look much like a guard dog right now, but the owner swore she was trained. Three more weeks those pups'll be weaned; maybe you can keep a couple and they'll train, too.''

Laura extended a loosely closed fist in the truck. The mother Shepherd sniffed, wary, and then slowly, lavishly washed her knuckles. She could have sworn the dog's eyes expressed mutual exhaustion for the patience required of all females in a dominantly male world.

"She's only two, and she's been treated right. We got her a house, the fencing to make up a kennel. Sam will take on teaching her the fence lines. You keep her penned during the day, set her loose at night. I'm not saying I was looking for a package deal like this but that's how it happened, and truthfully the pups will make it easier. By the time she knows the property the pups will be grown. In the meantime, she's not going to stray very far, and if you don't say something pretty soon, I'm going to get an ulcer. Are you angry or not?"

Laura intended to answer him. Soon. She couldn't very well yell and upset the puppies, could she? And the mother kept looking at her with those patient brown eyes, as if to say "the problems with males cross all species lines."

"Laura?"

She felt Nick's palm at the small of her back. His fingers slid up her spine to her nape, and the touch was a lover's touch, intimate, familiar, luring. Odd, that there was such a full feeling in her throat. "She'll never make a guard dog," she said finally.

"She will if you don't coddle her."

"That's easy to say. You know darn well I'll coddle her." She risked a look at him, trying to make it severe. "And Mattie's going to shoot you."

His grin was fast, once he saw the look in her eyes. "No, she won't. Mattie's never liked it that you were alone at night."

He didn't say that Mattie also thought the sun rose and set with him and wouldn't have argued if he'd brought in an entire zoo, but Laura already knew that was true. "Nick, you simply have to stop doing things like this," she said firmly.

"Like what?"

Like looking at her that way. She saw longing in his eyes. Every time he looked at her she saw need, raw and bold. She saw love, though he'd never said the word.

"Did you check out all you wanted to check out in town?" she asked him.

"Some. Hemming's covered his share of tracks in his time. And the man you fired . . . he seems to be spilling a lot of money in the bars that no one can account for."

"Which means nothing."

"Which means nothing," Nick concurred.

"And nothing's happened since I've been back, Nick. I told you that looking into both of them was silly. There never could have been a link to the incident in my hotel room and your pearls. New York's a huge city, for heaven's sakes. Things like that must happen all the time."

"Possibly." She didn't move when his palm stroked her neck. His thumb whispered along the pulse in her throat over her blouse. Her eyes dilated as if night had suddenly fallen, but she didn't move.

"I know you have your own work. It has to be suffering from your being gone this long. There's no reason for you to stay, Nick. I'll finish installing absolutely any security measure you want here, but we have to talk. If security is the only reason you've avoided talking about a partnership—"

"When are you going to tell me?" he interrupted her quietly.

"When am I going to tell you what?"

"What you're really afraid of, Laura." Gently, deliberately, he fingered the high collar of blouse, aware of her fast harsh intake of breath.

Her fingers closed on his wrist, but it was as if she'd touched lightning. Her hand trembled slightly just before she pulled completely away. He could almost see the shutter close down over her eyes. Her lips parted as if she wanted to say something, but she didn't. She strode for the house and never looked back.

"Those pups are wearin' you out, aren't they, love? Darn no account men. Have their fun and who pays the price?" Mattie crooned.

"I could have sworn you said yesterday the dog wasn't coming anywhere near the inside of the house," Laura mentioned dryly.

"What was I supposed to do? The poor thing came to the door all tired out. Soon as she goes back outside, those puppies just swarm all over her," Mattie said defensively.

"She's supposed to be a guard dog."

"It wasn't me that went to town yesterday to buy up every butcher's bone in the county for her. You're worse than me, and both of us are acting disgraceful. You'd think we never saw a dog before." Mattie sighed, then eased up off her arthritic knees. "Well? Where's the two of them now? Dinner was ready more than fifteen minutes ago. Nick's catching every one of Sam's bad habits and he's only been here seven days."

"I don't know where Sam is, but Nick was paying off the fencing crew."

"It all up now?" Fingers a blur, Mattie sorted through the silverware.

"Finished as of this afternoon." Laura poured ice water from a pitcher into the glasses at the table.

"He's a good man. Anybody else, I'd say it weren't right him setting up temporary house here with you alone. Silverwater ain't no San Francisco. People will talk. On the other hand, I saw just how he handled that Hank Shull yesterday afternoon when he came to call. Poor Hank looked like lemon jelly when he walked back out the door. I was wrong about him, Laura."

"I don't know why I'm asking this question, but wrong about who?" Laura straightened napkins.

"Wrong about Hank. He's nice enough, but he'd never have the sense to set up a siege. Maybe it isn't exactly proper, but the way I see it proper was probably never going to work anyway. When a woman's built up twenty-seven years of sheer bullheaded, maybe it takes a siege to make her see reason."

"I don't suppose I know this twenty-seven-year-old woman you think you're talking about."

Mattie was immune to sarcasm. "He worships the ground you walk on. And you look at him like the sun just came out after a rain. This is none of my business, mind you—"

"Absolutely none."

"But I see visions of a baby in this house within a year."

Laura's jaw dropped in mock horror. "Mattie, you're pregnant? And at your age?"

"And I ain't listening to no more talk about all this *business* you got together. You got one heck of a lot of cotton wool in your head if you think that's what that man is here for."

Compared to some nights, it was a mild lecture. Eventually Mattie always wore down and let the subject pass onto something else. Laura took hot pads and deftly removed the pan of lasagna from the oven. Usually she knew better than to argue, but tonight she couldn't resist one firm, "He's leaving soon."

"He ain't leaving you. I'm telling you that right now."

"He has a business practically on the other side of the world—"

"He ain't leaving you," she repeated.

"Mattie, could you kindly stop trying to marry me off long enough so that we could both eat dinner?"

"Well, where the devil are those two men?"

They came in less than five minutes later, and Laura knew the minute she saw their faces that something was wrong. Sam looked ready to slam a fist into the nearest tree, and Nick's eyes were coal-black and his whole body was panther still, panther tense. She looked at him and saw rage.

"The sheriff's going to be here after dinner, Laura."

"Lord, what happened?"

Sam said it. "People around here right and left and somebody still managed to walk in here bold as you please, drilled holes in the bottom of the brailer. It's sunk at the bottom of the cove."

Chapter 10

"Well now..." Sheriff Theodore Lanker scratched a straggly sideburn and heaved a sigh. Watery blue eyes squinted at the peaceful waters of the cove, washed in sunset. Then he looked back to the group on the banks. He hadn't had this much of an audience in a long time.

Little Laura Jakway was just standing there, still as a tomb, but then there was the foreigner—a big shot from the look of him, eyes colder than ice, and an anger radiating from him that Theodore just didn't much want to tangle with. Sam, Mattie Clinton, a crew of Laura's workers that must have come out of Camden, and his own two deputies were all waiting to hear what he had to say.

He quit scratching, hitched up his belt and straightened his posture so his badge would shine in the last of the light. "I can't see much more we can do here, with it getting dark and all. Fact is, Miss Laura, I don't much see what we can do anyhow. There ain't no tracks, no sign of who did what. Somebody obviously came in here by the river and sunk the boat, but any clues that might have been here are washed far down the river by now."

No one seemed too impressed with that judgment, which disappointed Theodore. He tried a hearty smile directed just at Laura. "Looks more like mischief than real trouble to me anyhow. You got a levy full of decent looking flat-bottom boats around here. Nobody harmed those. That brailer was old as the hills, you said it twice."

"Yes." Laura's voice was quiet and small.

"So, now. And you probably got yourself some insurance—"

She interrupted him when she stepped forward and extended her hand. "Thanks for coming, Ted."

When it came down to it, he was happy enough to leave, but the tall dark-haired stranger stopped him just when the group was breaking up.

"I take it that's all you intend to do about investigating this?"

Her visitor's voice sure did resemble ice in winter. "I don't know what more I can do, Mr. Langg. There ain't no clues to nothing, like I said. This whole town thinks the world of Miss Laura. Can't imagine anyone who'd want to do her a lick of harm. It had to be kids, a prank. And sure if I catch wind of something, I'll follow it through, but I'd be lying if I said I believed that would happen."

"Fine." Nick leveled the word like a bullet. "But I want one of your men around the property tonight."

"You mean all night?"

"I mean for the next few hours. I have to be gone for a short time and I don't want her alone."

"You think someone could still be around. Well..." Theodore watched his deputies already climbing in their cars, and thought about Bella's dinner waiting for him. "I guess I could sure enough stay for a few hours. Miss Laura's probably feeling a little nervous. I'll just call my wife—"

"Fine, you do that."

Trailed by Sam, Nick accompanied Mattie and Laura and Lanker back to the house. Laura flicked on lights and Mattie started reheating dinner as soon as she discovered the sheriff hadn't eaten. Laura had a coffeepot in her hand when Nick casually mentioned he was going to be out for an hour or two. Sam slipped out the door just before he did.

They both had fingers on the door handles of the pickup when they heard the kitchen door slam. Laura, arms folded around her ribs against the night chill, peppered down the back steps like a seasoned general.

"Neither one of you has had dinner yet," she said pleasantly.

"I promised Nick hours ago that I'd take him out for a pizza and beer," Sam told her. "It's been a long day."

"My hat, it's been a long day." She turned merciless blue eyes on Nick. "It's exactly like the sheriff said. It was just a prank. There isn't any other explanation. If anybody had wanted to do serious harm, they would have picked on my good work boats or my lab. Sam will be the first to tell you that the brailer was older than the hills and not even worth replacing.''

"I heard all that." Nick climbed into the truck seat and then lurched up so he could reach in his front jean pockets for the keys. Laura leaned over the open window like she intended to root there.

"So what's the sheriff doing in my kitchen, Nick Langg?''

"He's hungry, Laura.''

"And I have things to do.''

"You can do them with the sheriff there.''

"I've got a dog and a fence and Mattie hovering over me like a bat now. All for a kid's prank that never meant a thi—'' Her voice trailed off when Nick's palm gently smoothed back the hair on her white cheek.

"I won't go anywhere if you're afraid to be alone,'' he said quietly.

She backed away from his touch. "What I want is to be alone. Not entertaining troops in my kitchen.'' She directed to Sam. "You are not taking him down to the riverfront.''

Sam threw up his hands disgustedly. "Good God. All we're going to do is pick up a pizza and a beer. What's the big deal?''

"Nothing.'' She suddenly heard herself sounding like a possessive mother hen and abruptly backed up when Nick started the engine.

He waited until she was in the house before pulling out of the drive. "So.'' He glanced at Sam. "Where's this bar on the riverfront?''

* * *

He'd failed her. That thought kept attacking him as he found an empty parking spot near the neon sign that blinked HAR EY'S. The bar perched right on the river. The lot was full of aging pickups, and he could smell the choke of smoke and liquor even before they entered the door.

"The town's been trying to clean out this place for at least two dozen years. Never works." Sam slid both hands in his back pockets, sidling next to him. "Any place with river work draws its share of transients. Silverwater's a nice clean town, no trouble, no crime, nothing even open after nine. All in all, it makes more sense to keep a place like Harley's open. Like I told you, anybody interested in trouble—this is the only place they got to go."

He led the way and Nick followed. Inside, the place was lodgepole pine and no one had ever fussed with a lot of decorating. Bare tables filled up the floor space and a TV blared over the bar. Two women were paired off in the corner; the rest of the customers were men. Wisps of smoke hung at eye level like clouds and the smell of spilled beer dominated the room.

No one paid them any attention. Sam motioned toward the only empty table. "I'll get us a beer."

Alone, Nick straddled a chair, never bothering to take off his jacket. He saw a good share of week-old whiskers and a lot of beer bellies hanging over belts. He heard laughter and lazy, relaxed conversation. It was just a place for a man who had nowhere else to go, nothing to do. No one looked his way, or begged to be slammed in the nearest wall.

Unfortunately.

Nick rubbed the knotted muscles in his nape as Sam maneuvered around tables, bringing back two dripping mugfuls of beer. The beer was watered down, he could tell from the first sip. It also settled in his stomach like acid, but that he'd expected.

Although Sam had turned into a kind of Mutt and Jeff ally over the last week, he'd been more than surprised when Nick asked him to come with him. At first glance, Nick could see there was no point. A seedy watering hole was hardly going to yield answers when everything else he'd done had failed, but dammit, somewhere there had to be an explanation for everything that had been happening to Laura.

He'd not only failed to help her; he'd failed to protect her. He'd already done the logical things—the fence, the dog, the security system he was having installed. Laura had balked enough at those measures. She'd have had a fit if she really understood all he'd been up to.

He'd checked out every creep in town he could get the name of. She'd hired her share of derelicts in the past, but every damn one of them sang her praises. He'd spoken with townspeople she traded with. Everyone knew and loved Laura Jakway. He'd checked out what few men her name had been linked up with over the past few years, which had again raised a dozen questions in his mind about her innocence. But the main point was that she'd been squired around by nice men. A banker, a farmer, the local elementary school principal. Hell, they were all walking gentlemen.

He'd also had Nat Hemming professionally checked out, even to the point of visiting a man named Macklin in Camden—evidently a rival pearl grower the same age as Hemming. Nick had found out what he'd already guessed. Nathaniel Hemming was a shrewd, rich, private man. He gobbled up any property that had a lien on it. He had an ego bigger than all the outdoors. And he was a man who needed power to feel safe. Men like Hemming existed everywhere, but it never made sense that a wealthy man would risk petty crimes to hurt a woman who couldn't possibly threaten him.

He kept coming up with the same answers. No one wanted to hurt Laura. Maybe four incidents in three weeks was just remarkably coincidental.

And cats could fly.

The acid from the beer churned in his stomach. He'd failed her. In his mind, he could still see her face drain of color when Sam told her the brailer was vandalized. The only thing he'd been so sure of in the whole damn mess was that nothing would happen to her while he was right there on the property. Only it had.

Sam leaned forward and mentioned idly, "That's Simon Howard just walked in. The dude she fired. I told you about him."

Nick brought the beer to his mouth, taking a look. A pretty boy, he labeled him silently, with clean-cut looks and an engaging smile for the only two women in the bar. He swaggered toward the bar, raising a hand for attention as if he owned the world. Nick didn't need to give him a breath test to guess he'd al-

ready had a liquid dinner. He flashed a fat roll of bills
that had a few eyes pounce in his direction, and then
he turned with a beer, looking for a place to land.

When Simon spotted Sam, his chin tipped up in
wary defiance. But then he walked by, loping toward
the ladies.

"He needs his nose rearranged," Sam said flatly.

For the first time in hours, Nick felt a smile trying
to surface. Sam didn't live life in any complicated way.
If someone hurt you, you wasted them.

That wasn't Nick's particular life-style, but he
wasn't about to judge it. Particularly not now, when
helplessness was making him ache like a bad tooth.
Maybe helplessness could make any man turn a little
primitive, a little violent. But Nick didn't need a second look to know Simon Howard wasn't worth that
kind of energy. There was no way Howard had the
brains, skill or the wherewithal to have made that trip
to New York and vandalize her room without detec-
tion. He was too much swagger, too much braggart.

"I don't see any point in staying," Nick said tiredly.

"Might as well finish the beer."

He'd rather be home, building a nice locked tower
for Laura that only he had the key to. Sam, though,
had gone out of his way to be accommodating by
bringing him here. "Who else in the place knows
Laura?" he asked finally.

"Everyone. Five or six have worked for her, like big
Grady over there, and Carom. The rest all know her,
though. When she's taking on a river crew in the
summer, they'll line up to go with her before anyone
else. At least they did. Before Hemming decided to

deal with Silverwater's winter unemployment problem all at once."

"No hard feelings? No one with a grudge?"

Sam sent him a look. "Seems to me you know the lady. You picture her being mean to anybody without cause?"

"I can't picture her killing a mosquito, but that may be half the problem. She doesn't want to hear that half the world is filled with bastards."

Sam shook his head. "Take a look at the big dude over there, the one in the red shirt, all scarred up. Gordon's the name. Had a gas can explode on him two winters ago. Nobody could stand to look at him and she took him on. Fed his family that whole summer. He's bitter and he's mean and he was a no-good even before the accident happened, but he'd take out half this bar if anybody said anything against Laura. And if he didn't, I would." Sam swooshed down three long gulpfuls of beer, finishing his mug. He squinted at Nick, leaning back. "If the only reason you been sticking around is worrying there was no one to take care of her, I got news. The sheriff's always been a fool. When it comes down to it, that's only logical. This town doesn't have any crime worth spitting at. She's got other people besides the sheriff looking after her."

"There are other reasons," Nick said quietly, "that I'm here."

"Yeah, I guessed that. Just like I guessed you still haven't made up your mind about me, but that's okay. It took me a while to make up my mind about you. And in the meantime the two of us are talking real good and not doing a damn thing about what happened. Where the hell's that bartender?''

The bartender never had a chance to make it to their table before Simon Howard did, one of his hands holding a full beer mug and the other around a brassy blonde with more mascara than eyes. Nick took one look at the dare-me in Simon's eyes and mentally sighed. He wanted a confrontation. With anyone or anything. But not with a two hundred twenty-pound drunk spoiling to prove himself over nothing that had anything to do with Laura.

"Sam!" His voice was loud and slurred enough to make conversation hesitate at the neighboring tables. "Heard you been having trouble getting a river crew."

"You heard wrong then, Howard. We got ten times the river crew we ever needed, and every one of them twice as good as you ever were." Sam shook his head, smiling. "Pity I wasn't there the day you got fired. I would have liked mopping your face in the river."

"You and whose army?" Simon glanced at Nick, then back at Sam. "Glad to be out of that job. Hot work and nothing to show for it. That *bitch* is nothing better than a slave driver."

The room abruptly quieted down like a catacomb. "I'm sure I didn't hear you right," Sam said pleasantly.

"I'm sure you did. She thinks she can accuse me of being a thief and get away with it? And the news has already spread all over town that she had a little more trouble today. That's a shame, a real shame."

Nick said slowly, "Maybe if you leave real fast and real quietly I'll try to pretend that you never came over here."

Simon abruptly centered his focus on Nick. The lady next to him tried to nervously back away from his arm on her shoulder. "Well now, I heard about you around town, too. You wouldn't be the first dude licking after her heels, but like they say, once a whore..."

Nick caught Sam's eye, no more than a second's sharing look. "If you don't mind..."

"Hell, I don't mind," Sam said pleasantly. "You want to take time out to flip a coin?"

"No need." Even as he stood up, he knew that wasn't solving anything. Howard had at least thirty pounds on him, and his language was deliberately intended to provoke and incite. Nick was too old, too world smart and too worried about real problems to be drawn into some idiotic fight with an annoying gnat like Howard.

The young man did have a problem with his language, though.

And truthfully it felt good, damn good, to feel his fist slam directly under Simon Howard's chin. Simon went down. And faster than a bell could toll, all hell broke loose in the bar.

Mattie had long disappeared and Theodore Lanker had been yawning so often that Laura had insisted he go home as well. The kitchen and back porch lights had been left on for Nick two hours before, and by eleven, Laura had climbed the stairs to her room with a book.

The clock in the downstairs hall climbed twelve before she heard the dog bark. Barefoot, still wearing jeans and a gold blouse, she padded to the window. Her reading lamp made a glare so she switched it off, making it easier to see the yard below. Sam was shifting into the pickup driver's seat and Nick was already out of the truck and on his haunches, petting the Duchess and having his feet run over by puppies. Seconds later, Nick straightened, and the truck lights winked and dimmed as they backed out of the drive.

She waited then, listening for sounds that never happened. The back door always creaked when it opened. It didn't tonight. She knew Nick had come in because the on and off flick of lights changed the shadows in the doorway, but there was no clatter of hangers in the front hall closet when he put away his jacket. No bootsteps clapped on the black and white tiles below. No groan-like-a-ghost creaks were heard on the third step on the stairs going up, and a mouse couldn't avoid making that stair creak.

There was a vast difference between a man being considerately quiet and a man sneaking in. Laura was well aware she didn't have vast experience with men, but she happened to be in her doorway when Nick mounted the last step.

The night-light in the bathroom didn't illuminate much, but she could see that he wasn't wearing shoes. Also, his once-clean tailored shirt had a rip in the shoulder, was missing some buttons and hung out of his jeans.

"What on earth happened to you?"

His hand rushed up to the right side of his face as if he suddenly remembered an itch on his temples. "Nothing. Just went out with Sam for a pizza, Laura. Go to sleep." So pleasant. So cheerful. He yawned and moved swiftly past her. "Exhausting day. See you in the morning, honey."

Men! He undoubtedly thought he was home free. After all, she hadn't once entered his room from the time he'd been there.

She did hesitate in the hall for several seconds. He didn't close his bedroom door, but he didn't turn on the light, either. The boots he was carrying clunked on the carpet as he dropped them. Then she heard the smallest sound—a sound of pain—when the weight of the mattress gave beneath him. She moved forward blindly and from the doorway groped for the light switch to her left.

The light was bright, yellow, and less than flattering on the puffed greens and purples decorating his left eye. Guilt radiated from his right one. She said very softly, "Nick, I'm going to shake you so hard that your teeth are going to rattle," and then strode for the stairs.

It didn't take five minutes to accumulate a plastic bag of ice and the first aid box. By the time she returned to his room, Nick had pulled off his socks and was rotating his right arm as if there was some question in his mind that his shoulder was functioning. He stopped the instant he saw her in the doorway.

"Look, it's nothing—"

"Sam happens to be a small town brawler who I love very much, but I really thought better of you." Armed with the ice pack she advanced on him like a schoolmarm facing a truant. The pack was gracing his eye in a matter of seconds. "I thought you were an intelligent, civilized, responsible man. I could have sworn you weren't hung up on macho nonsense—"

"Laura?"

"What?"

"You're killing me," Nick said politely.

"I haven't even started." But once she'd checked to make sure his eye wasn't cut she let him hold the ice pack. "Violence, all violence, is disgusting. And at your age you should know that. Of all the stupid things to do." The side of his nose still had a spot of dried blood. Ever so gently, she used an antiseptic towelette and then reached for the first aid cream.

"Honey, it's not worth that."

"What happened to your shoulder?"

"Nothing." He added wryly, "But don't shake it just this minute, okay?"

"Look at your hand!"

"All it needs is a good wash. Which I'll do, just as soon as you—"

She did it. His knuckles looked like they'd hit a steel wall. The whole time she was rubbing a warm wash-cloth between his fingers, she kept thinking that he'd done this for her. He was a man who needed to protect and defend and from the very beginning, he'd been there for her. He was someone to talk to, to laugh with, someone to wake her out of the glass house she'd built of her world.

She'd been so selfish. From the day she met him, a simple and honest "no" had always stopped Nick. Honor and Nick were inseparable. She was the one who'd let the relationship develop that shouldn't have, and all because of selfishness. She'd wanted to be important to him, she'd wanted to love him. She'd wanted time with him on any terms she could have it. But Nick had fulfilled dreams for her—dreams of pearls and dreams about herself as a woman.

What had she ever done for him except hurt him?

"Would it help if I rubbed your shoulder?"

"Maybe...no...I honestly don't know. If you want the truth, I'm feeling like a total idiot at the moment and less than worth all this attention. You don't need to do this."

"Keep the ice pack on your eye." She shifted behind him, balancing on her knees on the bed. Until she knew if his pain was caused by a bruise or a pulled muscle, she couldn't be sure if rubbing would help. She touched, at first carefully, and when he didn't react with any pain, her fingers kneaded gently where he seemed to be most sore. "I don't suppose you're going to tell me where you've been."

His head was down and his voice muffled. "You suppose right."

"Did you learn anything you wanted to learn?"

"Sure. That I'm too damn old to act like a fool."

A smile curved on her lips, and then faded abruptly. "Everyone's a fool sometimes." She added, "This muscle of yours is as tight as a bullet."

"You should be on the receiving end."

"I think I could do better if you'd take off your shirt."

He juggled the ice pack from hand to hand while she unthreaded his arms from his shirtsleeves. After that, she seriously went to work stroking and kneading and pushing at the knotted muscle, but she knew the precise moment that he stopped talking. He tossed the ice pack on the floor, his spine straightened and his breathing changed.

His back was a long slope of gold-dusted skin, supple over sinewed muscles, taut over his shoulder blades. His collarbones formed hollows. She loved those hollows. She loved the bumps on his spine. She loved the warm male scent of his skin.

She loved Nick.

The muscle in his shoulder gave in and unknotted, and when that happened she let her fingers trail to his nape. The cords in his neck were tight, too, which justified her touching him there. Nothing justified her leaning forward and laying her lips in the hollow of his collarbone.

She closed her eyes and let her lips skim a line down his neck, trail down, then dance an unbroken kiss between his shoulder blades. Tears kept trying to swell in her eyes, but she was more conscious of another swelling, deep and huge inside her. *Don't risk this, Laura. Don't risk this....*

She had to. She seemed to have bound up Nick in feeling responsible for her. She also sparked needs in him, she knew that, and that he'd reached out to her in ways he reached out to no one. She hadn't closed that door in his face because of not loving him.

It was time he knew.

It was time she paid the price for those dreams of hers.

Dread was building up in her. It didn't help when her lips whispered across his shoulders and Nick abruptly sent the clutter of first aid equipment flying for the floor to clear the mattress.

She tried for humor, only because she wasn't sure what else to do. The words came out thick, like she'd just been swallowing molasses. "Are you going to pick up all those bandages?"

"Next year, yes."

"Look . . . I . . . maybe you're still hurting."

When he turned, she discovered that not even one badly puffed bruise could take the wicked black glint out of his eyes. "Never that hurt."

He eased off the bed and slammed off the overhead. Seconds later he switched on the bedside lamp.

She was staring at that lamp when one hundred-eighty pounds of half-bare male decided it had been nearly a week since he'd kissed her. The way he'd wanted to. Her hair feathered in his hands and he felt her beneath him as the weight of his leg slid between hers.

She could see in his eyes that it wouldn't be like the first time. That once he'd let go. He'd relinquished power and trust and control to someone else. To her.

Not this time.

The awareness in his fingers was sensitive to the point of raw when he freed the first button at the top of her blouse. He kissed her eyes closed. His lips moved to her hair, down the line of her jaw, back to her mouth. He unlatched the second button and the third and felt her body suddenly twist and buck beneath his.

He held her still with a leg pinning hers and a mouth that had no intention of severing contact. Slowly he let his palm sweep the length of her, cupping over breast, skimming the bones of her ribs, curling around her hip and holding her to him. He could feel the pulse of fire lash through her. Dim lamplight hazed color on her stark-white face when he eased his mouth from hers. She was breathing fast, but anxiety was coursing through her far more than passion.

His sore shoulder matched a belting pain beneath his left ribs. He was grateful for both. Pain distracted a man from sexual feelings. Laura's softness, her scent, her taste—nothing could totally distract him from the need starting to spiral through him in savage waves, but it did a little. Enough.

He took weakness where he found it. Her lips were becoming very weak. The feel of his palm courting the swelling ache of her breast through the blouse was another weakness. When his thigh gently rubbed between the cradle of her legs, a small sound escaped her lips. A weak, wild sound. She was so beautiful and while she was weak he stole open those last buttons.

"Nick—"

"Ssh." He parted the gold silk at her throat, and thirty-seven years of deprivation ached through him. He'd wanted to see her white throat for so long. The pulse, the hollow, the vulnerable skin. With infinite tenderness his lips pressed there, maybe inevitably diverted before his kisses began a long overdue quest.

The texture of her skin changed on the right side of her throat, exactly what he was looking for. The scar was the size of a knife blade and satin smooth.

"Nick—"

"Ssh." Her bra was the color of coffee and latched in front. Her breasts were straining to fit his hands the moment he freed them, and again he was inevitably diverted. The rosy tips pointed at him. At the softest lash of his tongue Laura shuddered. He nuzzled his cheek in that valley of softness and discovered he had a serious problem with fascination.

Her breasts were swollen hot, small and perfect, responsive to the least tenderness, hungry for the smallest attention. As a lover he savored that special vulnerability, explored exactly what touch of tongue and palm and taste could do for her, then stored that knowledge in his head for other times.

His features turned grave as he shifted slightly. He still didn't attempt to remove her blouse, only to push aside the straps and fabric that were in his way and Laura was suddenly breathing, breathing, breathing.

What he saw only confirmed conclusions he'd already reached. The clues had always been there—her fear of fire, the high-necked blouses, an inexplicable innocence in a woman who was fiercely passionate and giving. A more sensitive man would have reached those conclusions weeks ago. He'd never been at his most rational when he touched Laura. Now, even though he expected the scars, nothing prepared him for the well of rage that sang savagely in his blood at the look of her.

He guessed the burns had been deep enough to destroy nerve endings. The smooth tight skin banded over her right ribs, made a bar on the fragile right side of her breast, stole up to her collarbone and mapped jaggedly down her entire right side. What he saw was a blueprint of agony he hadn't been there to share. What he saw was a brand of pain that she'd imprisoned in silence for years. The fury kept building in Nick.

Laura kept trying to tug him up, move him, divert him. He wouldn't be diverted. His arm swept behind her and he lifted her so he could finish pushing off the blouse and bra straps still clinging to her shoulders, and the whole time his mouth was pressed to that...ugliness.

He wouldn't stop. He kissed her like he'd found something fragile, precious. He touched as she touched her most exquisite pearls. She couldn't understand. There should have been surprise. Shock. Revulsion. Instead, when he finally raised his head she saw fierceness and a graven anger in his features. His whisper was wild and low.

"I love you, Laura. Understand that, taste it, breathe it, believe it. I *love* you. I want you like no one I've wanted, need you like no one I've ever needed. I'll never let you go and you're never going to be alone again."

Tears were blindly splashing from her eyes when he stripped off her jeans, then his. When he thrust into her, colors washed over her flesh, the colors of heat and light, the colors of fire. Length to length and bare. She'd never expected to feel it.

Her breasts crushed to his sleek damp chest and her legs tightened around him, brazenly wrapping him tighter, wantonly locking him inside her. She'd lost every defense she'd ever held on to. There was only Nick, and he was being less than kind. He demanded...abandon. He demanded...yielding. He demanded a response from her that ripped loose everything she'd ever known of safety and sense.

They rode somewhere where blood was silver and the skies were hot. Where rainbows and lightning were one and the same. Where she lost Laura and became Nick. The pounding rhythm of intimacy—no one else could ever know it. No one else. Just her. Just Nick.

Chapter 11

I can't talk about it, Nick."

"Yes, you can."

The lights were off, the room all silver and black. Laura didn't know what time it was. They'd made love a second time but they still hadn't slept. She didn't really want to sleep, and Nick kept touching her. If he wasn't rubbing small circles at the small of her back he was gently, tenderly stroking her breast. Or her throat. Or her navel. Or anywhere. He neither ignored her scars nor paid any particular attention to them. At the moment he was half leaned over her and he said slowly, relentlessly, "Tell me."

"I don't want to talk about it."

"Yes, you do."

"Trust me, I don't."

But he wouldn't let it go. "What is it that you think that they mean? What is it you've built up in your head? I want to know. I want to know how you could possibly believe they could ever have made a difference to a man who loved you. They're scars. Nothing more. There's no possible way they make you less beautiful as a woman, less valued, less wanted, less needed, less loved."

"Nick—"

"We need to talk about the pearls, Laura. We have business to work out and we have to find an explanation for the trouble you've been having. We can solve those things." In the darkness his voice sounded like the rough edge of velvet. "But I'm not sure we can solve you and me. If you were another woman, I'd offer you wealth. I would promise you excitement, the excitement of different places and different things. I would promise that you'd never want for anything."

His thumb touched the pulse in her throat.

"But you're not another woman. And I'm a man who's never loved anyone, Laura. A man who's never shared. A man who's never had roots like the roots you value so much. I want your children. I'm terrified at the thought of your children. I want to make a home with you. I'm not sure I know how. And I want like hell to protect and keep you safe, to be someone you need and can hold on to—and everywhere I turn I've failed you up till now."

She twisted in his arms, leaning over his bare chest with a fierce blue glow in her eyes. "You've failed me at nothing. Don't you dare talk that way. I love you, Nick."

"I think you do," he whispered. "But I also think there was always more holding you back than scars,

Laura. Maybe it's simply me. The wrong man. You think I really don't know how little I have to offer you in the way of what you really want, really need?''

"You're so dead wrong." She showed him, the only way she knew how to show him. She showered him with kisses and wrapped him up. She took him inside her and simply loved him. All of him. Hook, line, sinker, heart, soul, cells.

For all the dreams in her life, she'd never once risked reaching for the one about happy endings. When she made love with him this time, she touched, tasted, lived that dream.

But at sunset the next day she found herself pacing the worn oriental rug in the library. The clock in the hall chimed seven. Both Mattie and Sam were gone. Nick had been in town most of the day. He'd returned an hour ago, only to ask her to hold dinner while he checked some measurements in the lab.

He was due back now. In fact, overdue. She had no idea what measurements he'd wanted to check. The dominant energy driving Nick all day had been in direct contrast to her own rare restlessness. She hadn't accomplished a darn thing, and her mood seemed to swing from elated exhilaration to a very odd, nagging and inexplicable uneasiness.

He loved her. She didn't doubt it. She didn't doubt that they would find a way to work out their different life-styles. She didn't doubt that they would ultimately find a reason for the incidents over the last few weeks. She didn't doubt that she wanted Nick's babies.

And she didn't even once doubt that she was going to have a ring on Nick's finger even faster than he'd pressed for it last night. Life had done a darn good job of teaching Nick that reaching out meant certain rejection, that love had to be an illusion for a man like him. She knew darn well she had a lifetime of work cut out for her, loving that man and loving him hard. There wasn't a chance on earth she would ever let him go.

Her pacing the library carpet had nothing to do with doubts about Nick. Something nameless, restless and painful had been chasing her all day. Nick had touched something deeply upsetting the night before. It *wasn't* only scars that had always held her back from commitment. She'd thought for years that it was. Only Nick had made her see otherwise. Scars, no matter what she'd believed, were only scars.

So what then? And why did it seem to matter so much?

She stopped pacing and leaned back against the desk, closing her eyes with exasperation. Too fast, too readily, images of fire danced in her head.

The phobia was old, tiresome and neurotic. Always, she whipped the mental images out of her head before they became too real. This time she didn't. Let it happen. Maybe then you can finally see how foolishly you've built up this fear.

In the far distance, she could hear the faint wail of sirens. *It's in your head, Laura.* She could smell the sweet scent of gas, when the gas pump was a quarter mile away by the lab. *Come on, Laura.* The last shimmering rays of the sun were really the only haze of light on her closed eyelids, yet she could have sworn an acrid wisp of smoke was drifting from the open west window. *Dammit, would you stop it?*

But her eyes blinked open when she heard an odd sound, like a hushed burst of wind in the distance. When she groped past the desk chair, its wheels spun behind her. The breeze was strong from the west. Her lab was to the west. The smoke was very real, and coming from the west. Nick!

Numbness hit as fast as the horror. He had papers all over the library desk. She sent them skimming, trying to find the telephone. The operator seemed part of the instant nightmare. She kept trying to say that the situation was under control. The volunteer truck and the sheriff were already on their way, even the fire department in Camden was already involved.

Laura dropped the phone. The déjà vu slamming into her heart stole every breath from her body. She'd known Allie Reese, the operator, all her life. In another time, another place, a million years ago, she could hear Allie's voice, reassuring her that a very different fire was well under control. Promises were cheap. She knew exactly how cheap.

Promises weren't good enough. She raced through the library, the hall, the kitchen. Outside, the steps tried to trip her, grass tried to catch under her bare feet. Something cut her right heel, and the old cottonwood and cypress blocked her view. It was worse when they didn't. As soon as she skidded past the trees she could feel the heat. A hot, shocking wave of it, and her chest was already heaving from the smoke.

"Nick!"

Licks of yellow flame were lapping a circle around the white stone building. The door to the lab was not only closed, but a long board braced against the knob. Smoke billowed in huge gray clouds everywhere.

It was the board that riveted her attention, not in the why or where it had gotten there, but in the awareness that Nick was locked on the other side. The lab had four windows. She might have been able to squeeze through any one of them, but not Nick. He was too big a man, the windows were too small. He *had* to get out through that door. As fast as she reached the porch to grab the board, another woosh of wind produced an explosion of flame in her face. She groped back blindly, coughing, smoke stinging her eyes.

"Nick!"

There was no answer from inside the lab, which was exactly when paralyzing horror engulfed her like the raw edges of a nightmare. This was it, all over again. The scars had never been the dream; her own burns had never been the terror.

It was this. No air. So hot. People she loved more than life in a trapped room. The nausea of smoke and nothing she could do, nothing that had ever made any difference. God, I can't go through this again, she prayed. You can't ask it of me. I can't bear this. I can't, I can't....

Even the sirens coming from the distance...she'd heard that siren of pain before. Sirens had never helped. Nothing had helped. All this time, she'd made so sure that she couldn't lose anyone else.

I won't love you, all right? I won't love you, Nick, I promise. I won't love anyone, only please, please, please...

She circled the lab, running, smoke sneaking into her lungs, crowding her nostrils, burning her eyes. There had to be something she could do. *I can't lose you, too. I can't. I can't.* Nothing was noisier than a fire, all wooshes and crackles and snaps. Through that, the sirens grew louder. By the time the fire truck roared in the yard, she'd dragged a wet fallen branch from the riverbank and was trying to beat at the flames near the door.

"Miss Laura!"

She wasn't listening. She didn't care. Someone tried to tear her away from the door. They were crazy. She wasn't leaving him. Only there was no air, nothing left to breathe. Someone kept snatching at her—like gnats those hands—and dammit, she couldn't see. How long had it been since she'd cried? Eight years? She didn't cry; she never cried. Crying never brought people back, and she certainly wasn't crying now, yet the sobs were choking her, blinding her, taking hold of her whole body and violently shaking it.

"Leave me alone!"

She heard a man's apologetic voice, a stranger's, and then she swallowed stars.

"Dammit, how hard did you hit her?"

"God, Mr. Langg, I feel bad enough. I swear she was going right into that fire if we didn't find some way to stop her. I just didn't know what else to do."

"You did fine. I'm sorry I jumped on you."

"You want I should give her a dose of oxygen? She had her share of smoke."

"No. Just leave me alone with her." Again, Nick rubbed the pulse in her wrists, then wrapped the coarse wool blanket closer around her chin. Night had fallen faster than the snap of a finger. The chemicals used to put out the gasoline fire still formed clouds and a stink around the perimeters of the lab. The fire truck's red lights were still turning; the stretcher Laura was lying on had come out of the sheriff's station wagon. "Enough, Laura. Wake up. Now."

First she felt the soreness in her jaw, which was as fierce as a toothache. Then she saw Nick's black eyes in the night as he leaned over her. She opened her mouth to try to talk, and then couldn't. She simply reached for him.

He held her, tight, fast, secure. "No! Don't even think it. It was a gas fire, Laura. A gas fire makes a lot of smoke, a lot of noise, but it fizzles out fast. Especially on a stone building. And you know damn well you had four extinguishers in that lab. It just took time to get it out, honey. No one was hurt. I wasn't hurt; you weren't hurt. No one was ever going to be hurt. How many millions of times have you told me that that lab was indestructible? Why didn't you believe it yourself?"

The volunteer fireman in a farmer's overalls and plaid shirt cleared his throat. "Basically, we've done all we can do here. Somebody will be back in the daylight to try and investigate the cause."

"No need for that. We already know how the fire was started. Talk to the sheriff. He'll fill you in. Just leave us be now, would you? And thanks for everything you did.'' He couldn't seem to hold Laura close enough. He wrapped the blanket around her and swung her up. He doubted she knew she was crying. Silent tears kept streaming down her cheeks like clear silver, like moonlight.

"Don't let go," she whispered. "Just for a minute more, don't let go."

She should be so lucky. He headed away from the noise and smells and confusion. As soon as he had her in the house, safe, warm, alone, he was going to let her have it for going anywhere near that fire. Maybe he'd even let her walk on her own, by next year. At that instant he wasn't all that sure what he was going to do with Laura except love the woman senseless.

"Mr. Langg!" Sheriff Lanker hustled behind them in the darkness, huffing and winded. "Everything we talked about this afternoon. It's all done, but especially after this if I could just talk to Miss Laura—"

"Tomorrow. Not now."

Sam caught up to them halfway to the house and fell in step. "She okay?"

"She will be."

"You sure?"

"I'm damn sure. But I'd appreciate it if you'd stick around until everyone's off the property."

The whole house was dark. He made her sit down in the kitchen, still wrapped in the green serge army blanket. He turned on the lights, reached in the closest cupboard for a glass, then groped for the brandy.

At some point when he was tipping the glass to her lips—she didn't want it—he took a good look at her face. Her eyes still had the glaze of shock. Her jaw was going to have a bruise. Tears had made interesting patterns through dirt and soot smudges. She'd never looked worse. She'd never looked more dear.

"I thought . . ." Her voice was hoarse and rusty. "I thought I'd lost you."

"That's never going to happen in your lifetime, Laura Jakway." He forced another sip of brandy on her. The color in her face was still ash.

"You were trapped in there. You were *trapped* in there, Nick, and I—"

"Once I used the telephone and played a little with your fire extinguishers, I took a very nice long coffee break in the bathtub of your lab bathroom. If you'll notice, I'm still a little on the damp, unkempt side. But that's *all* that happened to me, Laura." He added softly. "You were the one that had the trauma. And I would have died and gone to hell if I could have spared you that. You think I don't know how you feel about fire?"

She shook her head, blindly, wildly. "It's over. As long as you're all right. And I'm fine now."

He knew how badly she wanted control again. The damn light was glaring in her eyes. They were both filthy and exhausted, and all he wanted to do was hold her in any setting more comfortable than a kitchen. He never wanted to see her cry like that again as long as she lived. But the memories locked inside her had to be settled now.

"Don't you think it's time you told me about them?" he asked softly. "Your mother, your dad. You've been holding that grief in for eight years." He brushed the moisture starting to fill her eyes. "When you hold back grief, you hold back love, too. I think you loved them. I think you loved them like hell. I think you want to remember that love, Laura. I know it's hard, but can't you tell me?"

He would remember that night in the kitchen as long as he lived. Hours passed. Neither noticed. There was a point when Laura cried so hard he was afraid she was coming apart. There were also moments of laughter, when memories bubbled out of her one after the other—wonderful memories locked in storage too long, for two people that had meant the whole world to her. The rage of loss, feelings of unbearable helplessness, the loneliness. Grief wasn't a pretty emotion.

Sharing it, though, was the most intimate experience he'd ever had. Souls went on the line that night, not just hers but his. Love filled him up, so deep, so full, so rich. A man could damn well drown in all the love Laura had to give. Nothing, after that night, could ever be the same.

She not only woke up in Nick's bed, but found him wide awake and leaning over her. For a few seconds it was hard to think. Her head more or less felt as if someone had hit her with a baseball bat, and her jaw was sore.

Gradually she was aware of the pearl sunrise from the windows. She was more conscious of Nick's eyes glowing on her. There were shadows of exhaustion on his cheekbones. The swelling from his black eye had gone down, but the colors had turned particularly a vibrant violet and green. A night beard scratched his chin and his black hair was a mess.

She touched his cheek and smiled. So did he.

"Go back to sleep," he ordered.

"I love you, Mr. Langg. You're in so much trouble I can hardly believe it, but I do want you to know that I love you."

"Why am I in trouble?"

"You put me to bed before I even had a shower. Would you quit *looking* at me? I smell like smoke and dirt—"

"You do not."

"You're biased. Hopelessly," she accused, but then a light flicked on in her head and her expression totally changed. "Dammit, how on earth could I have forgotten what happened last night? How's my lab? Did the police find anything? How much damage was there? Lord, Nick, we have to—"

She would have leaped from the bed if he'd let her. He leaned forward to push her back where she belonged. Her hair was tangled from here to Poughkeepsie and he had a wonderful view of her bare throat, including the tip of one thin scar. His finger gently traced that scar. "Relax. The damage in your lab was not extensive. Nothing serious was lost. Your safe wasn't even touched. And yes, Laura, we know who did it. At this exact moment, the man responsible should be having his morning coffee behind some nice, solid iron bars."

"Who?" She almost cried the word.

"The man who set the fire, the man who vandalized your hotel room in New York, the man who put sugar in the gas tank of your pickup—it was all done by a loser named Ralph Baker. If it makes you feel any better, his job was to frighten and terrorize you—but never to directly do you harm."

"His job?" Laura shook her head blindly. "Nick, I've never even heard of him."

"Because he's not from around here. He was hired by a neighbor of yours." The expression in her eyes still looked bruised. His hands locked at the small of her back, insuring that she wasn't getting too far from him.

"Hemming?"

"Hemming," he affirmed. "Your neighbor had high hopes you'd run to him at the first sign of trouble and take up that business partnership he offered you."

"But all along, I never understood why he wanted that to begin with. Nick, he already has everything a man could possibly want. I was never any serious competition for him. Unless he knew about your pearls."

"He didn't know about *my* pearls. He knew about *yours*, and that was enough, Laura." Her skin was sleep warm and soft, and her breasts lay heavy against his chest. "You ran into a man's dream, love. It never had to do with money or even power. Hemming had a dream about being the best. He wanted his pearls to be the finest, the most valued, the most famed—not just in the valley, but anywhere, everywhere. He spent a life pursuing that goal. And he thought he had what he wanted until he saw your pearls in New York."

She frowned. "He bought my pearls," she said musingly. "He even showed them to me. At the time all I could think was that I didn't want him to have them. It never occurred to me—"

"That he was buying them to keep them out of sight?" Nick said quietly, "It took me forever to make the connection. I must have talked to every person who ever knew him from here to Camden. I had people checking on him halfway across the globe and back this past week."

"You never told me that."

"It wasn't doing any good. There were hints and pieces and clues and nibbles as to the kind of man he was. But it never came together until I finally came to some understanding of what motivated the man." Gently he stroked her hair, letting the silk untangle in his fingers, letting the weight sift softly through his hands. "I happened to know someone else who had a dream about pearls, love. Dreams that flawless pearls could make the nights less lonely, the days less long. Dreams that being perfect was important. Hemming, Laura, is a bastard who belongs in a jail cell, but like everything else in life, nothing is black and white. He let a dream go too far, become everything in his life."

She let the pad of her forefinger rub his bottom lip, effectively silencing him. "You don't have to be afraid I'll ever do that again," she said softly.

"No." He kissed the tip of her finger. "And I didn't bring that up to make you feel badly, but to explain why I'm no longer willing to use my grandfather's formula. You know from the heart how easily a dream can get out of control, and you happen to be made up of love and integrity and honesty and more love." He smiled, but the intensity in his voice was raw. "There are too many Hemmings out there with the wrong kinds of dreams. We could use our formula to produce perfect pearls for decades to come, but to do that we'd have to live behind a fortress, Laura. That kind of fortune has a price. It would never be possible to have a normal life."

"And that's what you want?" she asked quietly.

"That's what I want for you. Children playing on swingsets in the yard. People coming and going in whatever place you call home. Maybe a fence, but only to keep the dogs and kids in. And pearls. Honey, the last thing I want you to do is give up your pearls, but let's make them *your* pearls. All your pearls, created with your skills, invested with your pride—"

"Nick," she protested, but he was obviously going to continue on. She sent him a quelling glance, and then possessively smoothed back his hair, wondering when he was going to complain that her weight must be affecting his ability to breathe. "You're very good at figuring out what I want. How about what you want?"

"To build a bigger lab."

"And?"

"To watch you be happy." He raised his eyebrows. "Somehow I expected a definite argument out of you when we talked about the formula."

"Did you?" She felt the loss, bittersweet and fast, for those perfect pearls that would never be. She could also see in his face that arguments were useless. His mind was set.

So was hers. Any last lingering dream of perfection she'd been harboring had disappeared in the fire last night. Perfection meant nothing at all. Love did. Nick did.

To hell with the pearls.

"I'm still waiting for that argument," he mentioned.

"Ah, well. You can't have everything, Nick." She reached up, touched her lips on his and watched a man's very black eyes turn deep and soft. His night beard grazed her more tender cheek. In some other arena she was well aware that every muscle and nerve ending in her body felt sore, and all she could think of was that she'd misunderstood about perfection for a long time.

The feel of Nick's mobile mouth moving beneath hers... there was beauty. The gentle caress of his fingers on her bare throat... there was flawless sweet perfection. Nothing could be more exquisite than the love that flowed between two.

When she finally raised her head, there was a distinct masculine tension in his body that hadn't existed before. He shifted his legs. She knew exactly where he was uncomfortable, and there was a waiting strain on his features that tore at her heart. She whispered, "I love you, Nick Langg. If you want to know the truth, I love you in exactly the way that I've always been terrified of. I don't think I was ever afraid that you would discover my scars. Only that I would find someone I couldn't bear to lose, someone I needed too much, loved too much." She warned him honestly, "I'm going to be afraid of losing you for a long time."

"We could work on that. For a long time. Sixty, seventy years."

She wasn't in a mood to argue. She was more in the mood to stretch, languidly, making sure that a slight change in her position caused him maximum...discomfort. "Lord, you're going to be hard to train," she said despairingly. "You're overprotective. You serve champagne in swamps. It's a cinch you don't do dishes, and honestly, Nick. There've been times I've had to work terribly hard to seduce you."

There was his smile. A most wicked slash of a dominantly male grin. Then, in a room bursting with morning sunshine, he was wantonly peeling back the covers. "It's possible we could arrange things so you wouldn't have to work so hard."

"Talk's cheap."

"Talk's going to get you into more trouble than you've ever had to handle before."

"Promise?"

The sharp rap on the door startled them both. The voice on the other side of the door had the grizzly ring of impatience. "I looked up and down both sides of this property for the two of you, and since there's only one closed door and one bed been slept in I guess you're both there. Now all my life I minded my own business. Have I said one word about you two setting up house together? I ain't said one word and I ain't going to say one word, but I'm telling you now, I sure as heck hope someone's on the other side of this door talking about wedding rings."

"Mattie, if you'll kindly disappear we were just about to discuss that subject," Nick called out.

A moment's silence, while the dance in Nick's eyes met the laughter in Laura's.

"Just for the record, I'm taking the whole day off and locking the doors behind me. Don't you worry about a thing now. I'll kill Sam if he comes near the house and you just completely forget I was ever here."

They did, promptly. And as it happened, they passed an exquisite, intimate pearl of a morning.

* * * * *

*. . . and now an exciting short story
from Silhouette Books.*

*

HEATHER GRAHAM POZZESSERE
Shadows on the Nile

CHAPTER 4

Jillian had no idea how long the car careened through the twisting streets of Cairo. She was nearly unconscious by the time that it stopped; the exhaust fumes had penetrated to the trunk, and she felt cramped and nauseated.

She tried desperately to free herself from the blanket, but she accomplished nothing. Then rough hands dragged her from the car. She was carried—wriggling and screaming—for an unknown distance, and then things became worse. She was slung over the back of a creature that she identified by its scent and sound as a camel, and her misery grew. She could barely breathe, and every awkward step of the camel slammed into her anew. Once again she had no concept of time, nor could she comprehend any of the Arabic being spoken around her.

At long last the beast came to a halt. At a shouted command it fell to one knee, and again rough hands grabbed her. Still in her cocoon, she was tossed over someone's shoulder.

Suddenly she was cast to the ground, where she freed herself from the loathsome blanket. At last she could see! She was in a tent, but it was a tent unlike anything she could have imagined. It was beautifully appointed with silken draperies and pillows and exotic palm frond decorations. There was a low mosaic table upon which sat an exquisite coffee urn made of copper and brass, along with trays of dates and nuts and fruits.

"Welcome, Miss Jacoby."

Jillian gasped. Seated upon an ebony chair was the man with the scarred face. He was staring at her with an unpleasant smile, his teeth very white against the darkness of his features.

Jillian struggled to her feet. Who in God's name was he, and what did he want from her?

"Welcome," he repeated, and his smile deepened in a way that chilled her to her bones as he stood and came toward her. It was a ruthless smile, and Jillian turned to run.

She stopped quickly. The entryway was blocked by two very large men with evil expressions, and long swords belted to their waists. She heard the laughter of the man with the scarred face behind her, and she swung around, praying for courage.

"This is kidnapping!" she snapped, trying to appear confident. "I don't know what you want from me, but I'm an American citizen, and you can't get away with this."

"Fine. Thank you for the warning. Now where is it, Miss Jacoby?"

"Where is what?" she demanded in genuine exasperation.

"The film. The film for Achmed Jabbar."

She stared at him blankly. "I don't have any film. Not for any Achmed Jabbar or anyone else! I don't even know what you're talking about!" She forced a smile. "Honest to God. I'd give you your film if I had it, but I don't. So please, if you'll just get your goons to move away, I'll leave. No hard feelings. I'll just forget the whole thing. Now—oh!"

She broke off, screaming in sudden fear and pain. He had caught her elbow and twisted it cruelly behind her back. His menacing whisper just reached her ear.

"I can make you more cooperative, Miss Jacoby, and I can enjoy every minute of it. You're a very beautiful woman. All that blond hair and soft white skin." He released her suddenly, shoving her away from him with such force that she landed on the blanket. He smiled, stepping over to her again, pulling his switchblade from a fold of his burnoose. "It's American, too," he told her, indicating the blade. He turned it in his hands and smiled. "It can leave the most delicate ribbon of blood against your flesh—"

He broke off, because there was a sudden commotion at the entryway. He turned away from her, his burning gaze falling on the nervous newcomer, a short, squat man who spoke very anxiously and quickly. The man with the scarred face started to leave, then turned back to Jillian.

"Excuse me. I promise I'll return as quickly as I can," he said with cold menace. Then he left the tent, his guards behind him. Jillian quickly ran to the entrance, only to discover that the guards had not gone far. They greeted her effort with amusement, then took her arms and deposited her less than graciously on the blanket again.

Time passed slowly. Jillian alternately swore to herself and fought the tears of panic that rose to her eyes. She also ranted against Alex Montgomery. Somehow this was all his fault—she was sure of it.

Then she wished desperately that he were with her.

Darkness fell. There was no light in the tent, only whatever moonlight filtered through the translucent walls. Desolate and despairing, Jillian curled against one of the silken pillows, trying not to think of what might happen when her captor returned.

She was so exhausted that she started to doze, but then a slight flicker of movement caught her attention. She looked up. Silhouetted against the walls of the tent was the shadow of a man rising behind her. A scream caught in her throat, and she spun around, ready to do battle. Someone was coming toward her. Someone clothed in black from head to toe, moving silently, stealthily, toward her.

Suddenly he leaped forward and caught her, his hand swiftly covering her mouth.

"For God's sake, don't scream," a familiar voice whispered. "It's me!"

"Alex!"

"The same."

"Alex, you son of a—" she began, but her words faded away as she saw the relief—and the tenderness—in his eyes.

He smiled ruefully in the pale light. His thumbs brushed caressingly over her cheeks, and he asked tensely, "Did he hurt you?"

"No."

He lowered his head until his cheek rested against hers, then inhaled sharply. "I was so frightened for you. I'm going to kill that son of a bitch this time. If he had touched you..."

His voice trailed away, and he stared at her again with an emotion so intense that she felt as if she were melting. And then his lips met hers, and he kissed her with such passion that she actually forgot she'd been dragged into the desert and threatened with torture, and all because of some ridiculous roll of film she didn't even have. All she knew was the fever of his lips on hers, the sensual, sweeping stroke of his tongue, the hunger with which he touched her, and the sweet, desperate need he roused in her. She wanted him so badly. Her arms curled around his neck, and she wove her fingers through the hair at his nape, then felt the wonderful hot fusion of their bodies melding together. She felt ridiculously safe and secure, and deep in the recesses of her heart, she knew she was falling in love.

Love? How could she think about love? She was in this mess because of him.

Jillian twisted away from him, furious. "Damn you, Alex Montgomery! What in God's name is going on here?"

"I can't tell you now. We've got to get out of here. There's no time for explanations."

"Alex..."

But he was on his feet, as swift and agile as a black panther in the darkness. He laced his fingers through hers and pulled her along to the rear of the tent, where he had slashed an opening.

"You're no Egyptologist!" she whispered furiously.

"Yes, I am," he whispered back. "Now go!"

He shoved her through the opening, then followed close behind. She came out to a night alive with stars and a cooling breeze. In the distance she heard music and laughter, and she could see soft firelight outside a huge tent. She could hear camels braying and the snorts of horses, and smell the odors of sheep and goats.

"Let's go." Alex tugged on her hand. "Run. Now!"

She ran by his side, and together they reached a horse, a prancing, chestnut Arabian.

"Can you ride?" he asked.

"No!"

"Well, you're about to learn!" He swung her up, tossing her easily astride, then followed.

"Montgomery!"

The man with the scar was running toward them. But Alex didn't answer. Instead he dug his heels into the horse's flanks, and the Arabian reared, then galloped into the night.

Jillian turned to look behind them. Her hair flew across her face in the wind, nearly blinding her, and only Alex's embrace kept her on the horse, but she could see enough to be afraid. Scarface was now mounted, along with three others. And they were racing after Alex—after her—as they fled into the dark, never-ending void of the desert.

*   *   *   *   *

To be continued . . .
Join us next month, only in Silhouette Intimate
Moments, for the next exciting installment of
SHADOWS ON THE NILE.

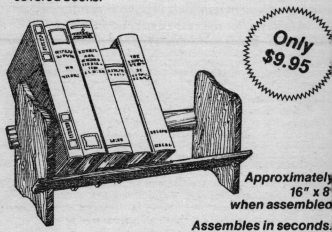

#225 STRANGERS IN PARADISE
—Heather Graham Pozzessere

Alexi came to Florida looking for peace and quiet. Instead, she found a house haunted by nighttime intruders. Her neighbor, Rex Morrow, was sure she needed protection, and her mind agreed, though her heart knew it would be much safer without Rex than with him.

#226 FANTASY MAN—Paula Detmer Riggs

Marshal Tatum Summers was falling in love with handsome Dan Kendall when she discovered he might not be as law-abiding as he seemed. She started investigating, determined to prove his innocence to the world, and just as determined to prove to him that they could have a future—together.

#227 WINDS OF FEAR—Margaret Malkind

Celine Conway had come to England on business, but she immediately found herself caught up in a whirlwind of adventure, intrigue and danger. Only Ian Evans seemed to know what was going on, but Celine wasn't sure she trusted him—though she knew she could easily love him.

#228 WHATEVER IT TAKES
—Patricia Gardner Evans

Sarah Harland thought Matthew Weston was her children's imaginary playmate, a substitute for the father they had lost. But Matthew was very real, as real as his love for Sarah—and as real as the dangerous secret he was keeping.

AVAILABLE THIS MONTH:

Silhouette Romance™

Legendary Lovers Trilogy

BY DEBBIE MACOMBER....

ONCE UPON A TIME, in a land not so far away, there lived a girl, Debbie Macomber, who grew up dreaming of castles, white knights and princes on fiery steeds. Her family was an ordinary one with a mother and father and one wicked brother, who sold copies of her diary to all the boys in her junior high class.

One day, when Debbie was only nineteen, a handsome electrician drove by in a shiny black convertible. Now Debbie knew a prince when she saw one, and before long they lived in a two-bedroom cottage surrounded by a white picket fence.

As often happens when a damsel fair meets her prince charming, children followed, and soon the two-bedroom cottage became a four-bedroom castle. The kingdom flourished and prospered, and between soccer games and car pools, ballet classes and clarinet lessons, Debbie thought about love and enchantment and the magic of romance.

One day Debbie said, "What this country needs is a good fairy tale." She remembered how well her diary had sold and she dreamed again of castles, white knights and princes on fiery steeds. And so the stories of Cinderella, Beauty and the Beast, and Snow White were reborn....

Look for Debbie Macomber's *Legendary Lovers* trilogy from Silhouette Romance: *Cindy and the Prince* (January, 1988); *Some Kind of Wonderful* (March, 1988); *Almost Paradise* (May, 1988). Don't miss them!

SRT-1